Kevin Ground is a third age author and spoken word performer. With a love of Ghostly Victorian Gothic, and contemporary horror crime fiction.

As a self-taught author, Kevin Ground has published essays, flash fiction, and short stories to anthologies of his own creation. Being well-travelled and well-read, he draws upon past and present experiences to create the characters and scenarios in his work. Re-imagining the everyday routine of life into unsettling, thought provoking stories.

This book is inspired by and dedicated to struggling parents everywhere. No matter their circumstances the vast majority strive to do their best for their children. All day every day.

Kevin Ground

BONECREAKE: THE STRANGE TALE OF MAUDY JILLER

AUSTIN MACAULEY PUBLISHERS™

LONDON · CAMBRIDGE · NEW YORK · SHARJAH

A CIP catalogue record for this title is available from the British Library.

ISBN 9781398456396 (Paperback)
ISBN 9781398462267 (Hardback)
ISBN 9781398463479 (ePub e-book)
ISBN 9781398463462 (Audiobook)

www.austinmacauley.com

First Published 2023
Austin Macauley Publishers Ltd®
1 Canada Square
Canary Wharf
London
E14 5AA

My wife, Lynette, is a constant source of support, encouragement and inspiration.

For her editing, proofreading and critique skills.

I am indebted to my friend, Sarah Chapman.

The winter of 1878 was notable for the heavy snowfall that laid a thick white blanket over the east coast of England and in particular the small hamlet of Bonecreake – a poverty ridden fishing community, straggling along the southern bank of the River Welland. At its juncture with the inland tidal wash and the cold grey expanse of the North Sea beyond. A forsaken place at the best of times. The bitterly cold conditions of this particular winter plunged Bonecreake into an unhospitable frigidity that no amount of scavenged driftwood could hope to enliven. While winter did its worst, anyone who called Bonecreake home, shivered and shook in their collective misery. Every scrap of clothing pressed into service – bodies shaking in the unrelenting cold that defied the heaviest overcoat and thickest shawl.

Those who could stayed close round their fires to wait out the freezing conditions. Those who couldn't for want of anything to burn froze in their own homes. Sometimes lying undisturbed for weeks, before the iron grip of winter eased enough for people to venture outdoors. Christmas that year was a desperate state of affairs all around. Cut off from friends and neighbours. Whole families spent the festive period wondering if their loved ones and neighbours were even alive. Let alone, celebrating Christmas.

Now it wasn't until the following spring that the story of Maudy Jiller came to light. Spring coming late that year as winter refused to relinquish its icy grasp. Until warm slivers of sunlight parted the skies of early March and finally began to prise the land free of the penetrating cold and snow. Starving and dishevelled, the surviving inhabitants of Bonecreake emerged from their cottages and hovels. Blinking in the first proper daylight most had enjoyed for almost five months. The previous autumn marked by near incessant rain and heavy overcast skies. A foretaste of things to come before the snow set in. Near waist deep in places. All about had endured a thoroughly miserable time of it and not a few had lost loved ones into the bargain. Lost being the word that played such a significant part in the tale of Maudy Jiller.

Of the 105 souls calling Bonecreake home at the beginning of autumn, no less than 27 had perished in the freezing winter cold. The bodies bought from their homes by their families to lie outside in the snow till proper arrangements could be made for a decent burial come the spring. There was no order to it. The snow being so deep, the departed ended up wherever they were laid. Close by the door they came out of in most cases. Lying in backyards and alleyways as grim evidence of winter's harvest. Now the survivors mindful that their loved ones remains frozen by winter's cold would soon thaw in the spring sunshine. Hastily summoned a clergyman and gravedigger from Braston. The nearest town of any size. Some fifteen miles inland from the coast. Informing them that their services were urgently required. It was when the mourning families began preparing their loved ones for burial, that cries of alarm and distress rose up amongst them. Of the 27 deceased awaiting burial, only 23 could be accounted for. To the horror of their mothers the bodies of four young children had disappeared with no trace of them to be found despite a frantic search of the hamlet and surrounding areas.

No one knew what to make of it. So in addition to the Clergyman and the gravedigger, a Constable was also summoned, lending the weight of the law to what was a desperate situation beyond the abilities of the simple folk of Bonecreake to comprehend.

The Constable, when he arrived the following morning, proved to be much younger than expected. A tall, energetic, clean-shaved man of slim wiry build in his mid-twenties named Hollins. Entrusted with the case due to a temporary shortage of more experienced men. The young officer was keen to show his superiors he was up to the task and advance his career accordingly. That being the case Constable Hollins immediately set about interviewing the families of the missing children. Slowly piecing together the grim circumstances of the children's cold related decline and subsequent deaths. When had they died? How had they died? Who knew they had died? Where exactly had their bodies been placed? All the while, further searches of Bonecreake and its surrounds, were organised and carried out under the Constable's methodical watchful eye. His organised methods reassuring the bemused Creakers as the inhabitants of Bonecreake were referred to by those from outside their hamlet.

Now being a great believer in gathering and sharing intelligence, Constable Hollins decided after his initial inquiries were complete and a working theory developed that a meeting with the local populace was required. The only building big enough for all to assemble in to hear the Constable's early analysis of the situation, was the three-sided rope shed. A long, low-roofed timber-built affair open to the elements at the front used for the storage and repair of the various fishing nets, lobster pots and canvas sail cloth used by the small fishing vessels that called Bonecreake home. The boats laid up for the winter alongside the rivers sloping bank. There amongst the miscellanea of the coastal fishing trade. Constable Hollins addressed the assembled Creakers. Standing in the entrance atop a small upturned barrel facing the anxious crowd, who found space to stand or sit where they could. The shadows of the rope shed pierced by the shiny brass buttons on his blue uniform as they shone in the faint snatches of sunlight breaking through the wind driven clouds. He was on the case. His chin up chest out manner reassuring to the bemused Creakers who waited expectantly. Compose yourself Hollins, speak clearly and make your audience understand. Squaring his shoulders and taking a deep breath he began. Speaking clearly in a deep baritone voice that belied his relative youth and slim build. Constable Hollins outlined the facts of the matter as he saw them. Slowly and methodically. As if speaking to a group of youngsters. A style best suited to the assembled Creakers, who ground down by the circumstances of poverty and unceasing toil were not over burdened with intellectual prowess.

"First of all I will confirm what you are already aware off. The bodies of four children, born and raised in this hamlet are missing." A stifled sob agreed from the shadows. "A distressing state of affairs to be sure but a state of affairs occasioned by the actions of someone yet to be identified." Here the Constable paused to draw breath and rock slightly

12

on his black booted heels. Mindful of the barrel beneath his feet not to rock too far and unbalance himself. "Not the actions of some snow spirit or any other strange wild creature sprung from grievous imaginings. Mark my words. Someone amongst you is responsible for this outrage."

Gasps and cries echoed round the rough wooden building and several women burst into tears of anguish. "No, this cannot be. For shame cried another, none of us here would be so cruel."

The young Constable let the crowd have its head for a moment or two before raising his hands before his chest. Palms down, patting the cold air in a calming gesture.

"Yes, I know it's a bitter pill to swallow but I can assure you it's the case. Now settle yourselves and I will outline the facts as I see them."

So saying Constable Hollins spoke steadily for the next 20 minutes. The assembled Creakers hanging on his every word.

"Now, as I said, I don't know who yet but I am convinced the perpetrator is close to hand. Bonecreake is 15 miles from anywhere and the torrential rains of autumn and heavy snows of winter have kept every road and cart track closed for months. The river has been unnavigable for the same reasons. Therefore it's good sense to assume only a person already in Bonecreake before the weather did its worst, is responsible."

Heads nodded in reluctant agreement amongst the pots and cordage.

"Now we can be certain the bodies were taken from outside four separate dwellings. Two from private yards. One from the street outside their front door and one from the outbuildings beside their home. I ask you. Who knows there way around Bonecreake well enough to gain entry to these places? Especially when every landmark is disguised by snow and frost."

"Only a local shouted a ragged shape from between two piles of lobster pots. Only a local echoed others taking up the cry." Their breath a white mist in the cold confines of the rope shed as the crowd grew more agitated.

Constable Hollins raised his hands for calm again.

"As you say. Only a local born and raised could find their way round, more than likely in complete darkness as snow or no snow. I am certain someone would notice a stranger digging around outside their homes. Especially as the missing were laid out reasonably close to hand."

For a few moments the Creakers stood silently absorbing the Constable's words. Brows furrowed in concentration until one amongst them voiced what several were thinking. "Why? Why would anyone in their right mind steal the bodies of our little ones? Heaven knows children go missing in towns and cities for a variety of reasons but here."

The question hung in the air unanswered. One of many Constable Hollins had to deal with. From his initial investigation he already knew, Bonecreake was so small half the crowd was related in some way to the other half and the idea of stealing a child belonging to your own family seemed complete madness.

Constable Hollins kept his sharp blue eyes on the crowd as they looked at each other. Bewilderment, fear, the sprouting seeds of suspicion, all present in tear-streaked faces. These were people used to doing. Labouring long and hard to scratch a mean harvest from the river and sea estuary beyond. Capable and steady in their own ways. Now hamstrung by a

14

situation beyond their experience where they could do nothing. They became a slow bubbling pot of emotions liable to boil over in fear and frustration. Constable Hollins bided his time, waiting to see what would rise to the top as the crowd fidgeted and cast furtive glances left and right.

It was but a minute until the Constable spoke again but for the Creakers, it seemed like hours. Lost in their own thoughts before the deep baritone voice bought them all sharply back into the reality of their situation.

"One of you asked me a question that seems most relevant." The heels of the Constable's highly polished boots, rocked slowly easing blue uniformed knees. "So I will ask you all the same question but in two parts. Firstly, are you all here? Look around you now. Can you account for your friends and neighbour? Is anyone missing who hasn't been seen since winter eased and the children were found to be missing?"

The assembled Creakers immediately began looking about them, voices raised, questions asked till the Constable drew them once again to his attention.

"Secondly, is anyone hiding anyone away? A family member kept behind closed doors when they should have been committed to the local bedlam for everyone's safety. Someone possibly capable of these unspeakable acts whilst gripped in a fit of madness?"

Gasps and cries rose from the between fishing nets and piles of lobster-pots. Echoing around the rough timber planking.

"Dear God, a maniac hidden amongst us moaned one. A madman on the loose groaned another." The Creakers positively shook with fear and confusion as Constable Hollins sharp eyes watched and waited for any development. Anything he could use to further his investigation.

"Old Tom," the name shouted from somewhere among the crowd stilled the babble of anxious voices.

The shaking figure of a woman swathed in a ragged assortment of whatever she owned to keep the cold out, stepped forward from the shadows and pointed a stubby finger at the Constable's brass-buttoned chest. "Old Tom isn't amongst us." Her voice broke into a sobbing cry as Constable Hollins identified her as one of the mothers missing her child. Shuffled to the front of the crowd. The weeping mother collapsing at the knees to sit astride a pile of rolled fishing nets.

"He's not here and I haven't seen him anywhere since we began searching for our children." A flood of tears finally rendering her speechless as several other women gathered round her to offer comfort and support. Amongst the Creakers a hubbub of noise exploded once more. The boiling pot of emotion so keenly observed by Constable Hollins, spilling over as the Creaker's cast about them for the missing figure of old Tom. Each questioning the other. "Have you seen him? No. Have you? No, not I. Nor me."

From amidst the chatter and searching eyes it was confirmed old Tom was not amongst the small crowd and no one had lain eyes on him for a good while. Certainly not since the children had been declared missing. Quickly Constable Hollins took charge of the situation. His voice once again steadying the Creakers.

"I will take two of you with me. You. The ragged figure of a tall woman swathed in an assortment of shawls started in surprise and you. A heavily-bearded man of middle years stepped forward as the Constable addressed the Creaker's once more. It will do no good all hands turning up on this man's doorstep. The rest of you go on about your business. If there's news to be shared, rest assured you will be told as quickly as possible. For now let me investigate further. The Constable motioned towards the open end of the rope shed. Lead the way if you will and let's see if this old Tom is to be found."

"Choose someone else the tall woman demanded. Her voice vibrating in her chest to give her words a strange rattling quality. I don't want to go."

Constable Hollins worth stared hard at the skeletal figure. "Take a firm hand, Hollins. Once a crowd see's someone dispute your authority, they'll all be at it. Bully them if you have to but retain control at all times."

"Yes, sir."

"But go you will and that's that. You will be my runner if more support's needed." The steel in the Constable's voice brooked no argument.

"Now. Let's be about it."

With a curt nod of dismissal to the assembled Creakers, Constable Hollins followed the two chosen to assist him out into the thawing snow.

****

"I have lived here all my life," the bearded-man answered when questioned by the Constable as the trio walked steadily along the rough, slush strewn track towards old Tom's cottage.

17

"Isac Punce is my name. I have fished the wash and sea beyond for nigh on 30 years."

"A hard profession commented the Constable, keeping step side by side with the man as he talked." Voice muffled somewhat by a cold biting wind blowing straight of the river catching words as they were spoken and throwing them into the air.

"I do not find it so," answered the fisherman. "In the winter months I rest because the weather will allow me to do no other but on a summer's morning with the sun on my face and open skies above, it's as near a pleasure as work can be. Those left ashore like Maudy here have it harder."

The Constable turned his attention to the gaunt, rag swathed woman leaning into the wind as she marched along in a pair of heavy man's boots. Skirts held above the muck and puddles of the rough track by broken nailed hands. Clutching the material tight lest the wind steal it from her grip.

"Tis true enough." She agreed, the curious vibrating quality to her voice rattling against the wind. "Life is hard and gets no easier as the years take their toll of youth and strength."

"Then why do you stay inquired the Constable. There's better paid work to be had in the towns nearby and willing workers are always wanted?"

The woman snorted through irregular yellowed teeth. "I'll not be taking me or my two little ones to no town, where I work all day to make others rich while spending my nights fending off the unwelcome advances of any rascal who wants to take advantage of a woman alone. No Bonebreake's my home and there's work enough here to earn my keep without being pestered by every man seeking an opportunity to pleasure himself at my expense."

"I see," answered the Constable as a particularly violent gust of wind fluttered the material held tight in her grasp. "You live alone?" He probed gently, taking the opportunity to gather a little more background information about the residents for investigative purposes.

"I do," answered the rattling voice. "These four years since my husband passed away. God rest his soul. Me and my two girls don't need anyone else. We do for ourselves and manage with what we have."

Looking at the woman's gaunt hollow-eyed face, blue lipped in the cold wind. Constable Hollins could only conclude that whatever the small family had to manage on. It seemed little enough to sustain them.

Maudy Jiller. For that was the woman's name, stopped and pointed at a row of three small, single-storey, stone-built thatched-roofed cottages, sitting slightly back from the track. Old Tom's being in the middle of the row. The cottages either side leaning towards the centre for support, both unoccupied and showing signs of dereliction.

Constable Hollins took a few moments to assess the situation. Running likely scenarios through his mind while he questioned his two companions about the as yet unseen old Tom.

"Grumpy old bugger most of the time. Volunteered Isac Punce. Don't recall him being over friendly with anyone. Was said hereabouts he used to earn his living fishing but I never seen him take a boat out. Like Maudy here, old Tom does what he can where he can. Lived alone in this little place for years."

"I never took to him." Maudy Jiller's voice echoed from the depths of her chest to vibrate in her throat. "Always thought he was a bad un hiding himself away amongst the innocence around him."

Both the constables and the fisherman turned against the wind to stare at the woman.

"Why do you say that, Mrs Jiller?" The Constable's nose, red-tipped in the cold wind positively quivered at the scent of something amiss?"

"Well, he wasn't born in these parts for a start and he was always cagey about where he came from before he settled here. Fond of the bottle as well. Stunk of drink most of the time. I never liked to be around him. Always looking at me funny. Eyeing me up for a bit of mischief I shouldn't wonder."

"Well. I think its high time. I made the acquittance of old Tom whatever his faults might be."

The Constable squared his slim shoulders and walked the six steps from the track up the slightly rising stoned path to the front door of the middle cottage. Briskly rapping his knuckles against the weather-stained unpainted door to announce his arrival. His two companions bringing up the rear. Once, twice, three times the door rattled under the knocking but to no avail. Old Tom, if he was at home, wasn't receiving visitors. The door firmly bolted shut.

"Is there another entrance?" inquired the Constable?

"Round the back," answered Isac Punce turning to lead the way back down the path and around the side of one of the abandoned cottages. "These old places share a yard and a privy. They have back doors so you can come and go as you please."

Moments later the unlikely trio arrived at the back entrance to the cottage. Just as Isac Punce described the shared, wood-built privy sat shed like, square in the middle of a shaded snow-covered yard. Three back doors faced out onto the same yard. Two outer doors tight closed. The middle door of old Tom's cottage slightly ajar. Snow piled against and through the opening raising concern within the Constable's mind.

"Right, you two." Constable Hollins stopped his companions as they were about to walk across the backyard. "Stop. If I need you, I'll call out. Otherwise stay back. This is police business and I don't know what I might be walking into. So for your own safety wait here."

Without waiting for any argument he strode across the small yard. Snow crunching beneath his boots. Eyes everywhere, taking in every detail he could see, which was little enough due to the snow still lying above the top of his boots. Especially in the deep shade by the cottage doors. Pausing by the slightly ajar door Constable Hollins strained his ears for any sounds of life. Before slowly pushing against the door, which surprisingly swung open on well-oiled hinges. The single room beyond in complete darkness.

"Hello, hello," bellowed the Constable. Startling his waiting companions as his deep voice boomed back at them from the stone walls of the cottage. "I am Constable Hollins. Here on police business. Show yourself or I shall be forced to enter." The Constable's heartbeat loud in his chest as he steeled himself for he knew not what to come hurtling out the darkened room. Behind him Maudy Jiller and Isac Punce stood tense as bowstrings caught up in the suspense of the moment. The Constable up to his ankles in the snow silhouetted against the dark doorway. "Right. I'm coming in," shouted the Constable taking a tentative step over the threshold. Cautiously minding where he stepped. Aware clues might be under foot blanketed in darkness. As might items of furniture, old Tom or four dead bodies. "Light," he muttered, "I need light." Carefully shuffling close to the back wall he moved sideways until he reached the small window built into the wall. Moments later in a cloud of stifling dust, the rough sacking used for curtaining was pulled aside and what little daylight was in the shaded back yard lightened the gloom, enough for a very nervous Constable Hollins to see right across the single room. He wasn't alone. Built into the stonework of the dividing wall between this cottage and the one next door, an open fireplace stood bare and empty. To one side of the open hearth as if warming his feet by the fire, old Tom or what was left of him sat at his ease in an old rope backed wooden armchair. A good head of steel-grey hair and heavy mutton chop side whiskers of the same colour, framing a wrinkled face sunken over skull bones in a grim death mask. Hands like shrunken claws gripping the chair arms as if old Tom had known he was slipping away and held on tight as long as he could to this mortal life. Both eyes frozen in time as they stared sightlessly into the bare fireplace.

The tension and fear in Constable Hollins came out of his body in a gasp, loud in the still room. "Well, at least I know why you didn't answer my shouts." Observed the Constable Wryly. Standing perfectly still by the window. Eyes taking in everything. Searching every corner. Looking for what might be missed if he moved in haste. Finally satisfied, he walked six careful paces across the room and pulled down the sacking from the front window, allowing the unshaded daylight at the front of the cottage to flood the room with light. It was a grim scene laid out before him. The room itself, empty of all furnishings save the chair occupied by old Tom's remains. The hard earth floor and stone walls completely bare of ornament or miscellanea of any kind. Only a selection of brown spirit bottles, uncorked and empty lay at the corpse's feet. Testament to Maudy Jillers assertion that old Tom had a fondness for the bottle.

"Constable," the shout from the waiting figures in the yard startled Constable Hollins from his reverie. "Constable, is all well?" Isac Punce's shouted against the blustery wind outside. "Well enough," the Constable responded turning about to walk across the room to re-appear through the back door. Just as his two companions hurried through the snow towards the cottage. An expectant look on their faces.

"What news," demanded Isac Punce. "What of old Tom?"

"Well, not much to tell at present." The Constable pulled the back door closed behind him as he made his exit. The cold shade of the backyard adding extra venom to the biting wind. "Old Tom is dead and his remains lie within."

A low breath escaped from Isac Punce. "So that's why he isn't to be found then? The colds took him." The Constable led the way back across the yard and round the side of the small row of cottages.

"It would seem so, yes. But I will return with a lantern and have a good look round before we disturb the remains. In the meantime we will inform the rest of the village that old Tom has passed away and no trace of the children have been found about him."

"Another unfortunate soul sacrificed to winters cruel harvest it would seem." Isac Punce trudged through the snow and slush. "Pity. He always looked well despite his years."

"Well, be blowed, Isac Punce." Maudy Jillers voice carried a vibrating edge to it as sharp as the cold wind blowing in off the wash. "You can't tell the difference between a rosy cheek and a drunkards flush. He was always as red as a berry because of his love of strong spirits. Shouldn't be surprised if he didn't drink himself to death long before the cold got to him. If you've pity to spare, don't go wasting it on the likes of him."

At this Isac Punce muttered through his beard and shook his head.

"It does you no credit to speak ill of the dead Maudy. Old Tom's gone, let him lie in peace. Whatever his faults we have other fish to fry."

"Fish to fry," he says. "Maudy Jiller bit back viciously. Chance would be a fine thing, Isac Punce. There's been no fish to fry in Bonecreake these last five months and not liable to be unless you and others like you bestir yourselves to make use of the spring tides."

Unperturbed Isac Punce splashed along the sodden track back to the rope shed. "Shout at me all you wish, Maudy. My shoulders are broad and I know you too well to take offence at your sharpness."

Maudy Jiller pursed her blue lips even tighter but made no further comment as the trio finally reached the rope shed and the quickly assembling villagers who had waited there for news of old Tom. Hoping against hope for answers, only to be denied as word quickly spread of old Tom's demise.

"Can't have been him then. No. Who then?" The question hung over the Creakers like a mist of desperation impervious to the gusting wind.

"What now? Then Constable was the question on most lips. Where to? What to do?"

Constable Hollins's answer held little comfort to the families of the missing.

"I shall continue to investigate and see where my investigations lead. In the meantime, stay calm."

"Calm," he says, calm. "The gravedigger and priest will be with us on the morrow and still no sign of our little ones."

"That's true enough and more the pity," responded the Constable. Voice firm and clear. "However, the two you speak of have plenty to keep them occupied for a day or two and you all have a living to earn now winters eased. So I suggest you go about your business and apply yourselves to putting food on the table. Enough have already fallen foul of hunger and illness through the winter. Don't let the same be said of springtime."

That steadied the crowd. The Constable's carefully chosen words gave them purpose over and above the need to find the missing children. The ice and snow no longer held the river and wash in its grasp and they were, after all, fishermen with mouths to feed and money to earn. Life despite their situation had to go on.

Later that same day, armed with a bright lantern, Constable Hollins investigated every shaded nook and cranny of Old Tom's cottage. On his knee's shuffling slowly across the hard packed soil floor, peering into corner and fireplace alike. From the moment he'd entered the cottage earlier in the day, something had vexed the Constable. Something he couldn't put his finger on until it suddenly dawned on him. Old Tom had lived in this cottage for years. Isac Punce had said as much, so where was old Tom's furniture? Where was his clothing and bits of pieces of his life? The plates, cutlery and cooking pot? One would expect to find even in the meanest of homes? Candles, matches, oil lamps and firewood? Gone? All of it? Not a scrap to be seen. Even the rope netting that would have held his straw mattress off the floor. Gone. As was the mattress and bed frame. If old Tom hadn't sat dead in his armchair, there would be absolutely no trace of the man to give a clue that he had ever been there at all. All of which posed the question. Had old Tom sold his furniture and effects for the price of a bottle or two of spirits. Or had someone stolen every stick of furniture and all he owned while the old Tom sat idly by and watched on? One scenario as unlikely as the other.

"The children, Hollins. What about the children?" The voice of his superiors sounded in his head as he sat back on dusty knees and considered the evidence or lack of it before him. Brain running fast and sharp as bits and pieces fell into place. A gentle humming in the background as concentration gave its self a voice through his pursed lips. The lantern bright as the sunlit day began fading into an overcast late afternoon. The chill of the room unnoticed as he immersed himself into every aspect of the case. Finally shaking himself to stand stiffly upright as cramp began to stiffen his calf muscles. Small puffs of dust rising from beneath his boots as he stamped his feet to restore his circulation.

The bare room had yielded no answers but the quite had given clear thought, space to flourish. Unfortunately for the stamping Constable, his musings had produced more questions than answers.

"A pity you've nothing to say." Constable Hollins stood over the semi frozen, mummified remains of old Tom. Not a big man to begin with. The corpse sat silent and shrivelled in the armchair. Skin like grey parchment stretched taut over the sunken features. Dressed in a collarless shirt and grey sail cloth trousers. The trousers much stained. Especially around the crutch where old Tom's shrivelled backside met the straw filled cushion, sitting on the armchairs solid wood seat. Looks like you couldn't make it out to the privy in the end. Too drunk, too weak, dying in your own filth. Constable Hollins shook his head sadly. No way for any man to end his days. It's only the cold that's saved you from rotting away completely. Sightless eyes stared back at him from the shrivelled face. No answer forthcoming. Which was a shame for old Tom had seen much and had a tale to tell which he would take to his grave. That would have led the young Constable straight to the missing children and the architect of their disappearance.

As it was with little to work on and no further information forthcoming. Constable Hollins spent the early part of the evening sat in quiet contemplation. "A small fire warming the room where he had set up temporary lodgings, casting long shadows over and around the seated man. Eyes closed, lips slightly apart as every ounce of knowledge, every feeling and emotion was sieved through a fine mesh till the fire burned low and the shadows faded into near darkness. Sat on a low wooden stool in his shirt-sleeves the Constable knew more about Bonecreake and its inhabitants than the Creakers themselves and yet nothing had come of his ruminations to suggest a way forward. No inspiration at all until a small piece of ash shifted slightly in the fireplace. Instantly the Constable's blue eyes opened, piercing the stalemate of his thoughts with one starling question. Evidence. Old Tom's cottage had been stripped bare to remove all evidence of wrong doing. This wasn't simply a question of someone stealing the old man's possessions. Someone had actually used the old man's home as their own. Either while the old man was alive or after he was dead. He had no family, no close friends. Indeed if Isac Punce was to be believed old Tom was an irritable unwelcoming man. The empty bottles backed up Maudy Jillers assertions of an unsociable man who liked to drink. Yes, everything except the body and the armchair had been stripped out of the cottage, leaving no trace of anything. Soil floor swept clean and the fireplace emptied of ash and brushed clean. Any connection with the missing children had yet to revealed. If it existed at all but that cottage held the key to something. Come daylight I'm going to find out what spoke the Constable. Standing and stretching before bending to light a candle from the glowing embers of the dying fire. An early breakfast and out the door at first light. Much to be done," he muttered throwing another log or two onto the embers, to warm him through the night. ? Much to be done his last thought as he laid back across his temporary bed and fell almost instantly asleep."

****

The morning dawned cool yet fresh with a hint of spring warmth as the Constable. True to his word was up and about before most were even awake. Rousing the Creakers to assemble a team of eight people to accompany him to the group of cottages on the edge of the hamlet. On arrival old Tom's body was lifted respectfully as possible from his armchair and taken to the small cemetery plot in a wheelbarrow for a decent burial at the grave digger's convenience. The remaining seven members of the Constables assembled group. Five women and two men. Isac Punce among them listening intently to the Constable's instructions, before setting to with a variety of sweeping brooms and shovels to clear the yard at the rear of the cottages off any remaining snow and slush. The day gradually warming around them into a fine bright morning. Either side of old Tom's cottage the two derelict cottages were carefully entered by Constable Hollins and Isac Punce. Neither was found to be of any interest. Both bare and badly in need of maintenance. Long since abandoned to the pigeons and vermin living in the sagging thatch. The yard proved to be of no use either. Beneath the snow the hard packed earth yielded no clues. Nothing to suggest anything out of the ordinary. A thorough search of the small front garden proved fruitless and the Creakers were beginning to lose hope when the Constable ordered a short break in proceedings to take stock. The small group standing in the warm sunshine bathing the front of the cottages. Two of the women retiring to the rear to use the privy while the others lounged with their backs against the warm stone. Constable Hollins slightly apart from the group, deep in though. Brass buttons shining in the sunlight. Aware he was keeping the Creakers from their work and the desperately needed return to the normality of life. If ever such a thing was to grace Bonecreake again.

"Do you think we…" Isac Punce's inquiry was cut short as a muffled scream came from the rear of the cottages and hurrying footsteps announced the arrival of the two women. Who came flying out of the front door of old Tom's cottage in a flurry of shawls and skirts. Colliding with the burly figure of Isac Punce as he jumped smartly to his feet in alarm. As might be imagined the next minute or two was bedlam as the startled Constable sought to restore order. The burly fisherman and two frightened women all a tangle, as the rest of the group looked about them in shocked confusion. Drawing away from the cottage door lest some menace suddenly appeared from within to threaten them. "Ladies, calm yourselves, please." The Constable employed his palms down, pat the air approach as the two women disentangled themselves. A mixture of fear, panic and embarrassment writ large on their faces. The group standing around them open mouthed in anticipation.

"It was a rat!" Exclaimed the younger of the two women.

"Aye, that's right." Agreed the other. "A bloody big rat in the privy. I fetched the seat a kick or two in case anything were nesting down the hole and this bloody great rat shot out while I was getting myself ready to go. Christ, it's a mercy I hadn't sat down without checking."

"That's not all," shouted the younger woman. "It was a big un and no mistake but it was all sticky like."

"Sticky." The word hung in the air as the group drew closer round the frightened women. "How so?"

"I mean round its mouth and its whiskers. Bits of something stuck to its whiskers. Horrible it was. Big fat and horrible." The woman shuddered at the recollection.

"Was it just the one?" asked someone in the group. "There's usually more, see one, see another. I hate rats."

"Me too. Can't abide the bloody things."

"All right, everyone. Let's give these ladies some air. You're all pressed in so tight there as like to suffocate before much longer." The Constable as shaken as the rest of them stood back at his own direction as did the rest of the group. The frightened women vowing to hold their water till their husbands had checked their own privies at home.

"Funny thing though." Every head turned to the younger of the two women. "I didn't know rats ate shit."

In an instant Constable Hollins was all attention. Grasping Isac Punce by the arm and wheeling him about. "With me, Mr Punce. Bring the lantern from inside the cottage if you, please. This incident requires further investigation."

To a casual passer by the scene would have appeared strange to say the least. Armed with a shovel and lantern, the burly fisherman and the Constable approached the privy with caution. Behind them, huddled together the rest of the party minus the two frightened women stood ready with brushes and sticks. The fisherman with the Constable at his shoulder slowly eased open the wooden privy door which opened with a dry hinged groan. Seconds later the shovel banged against the top of the raised wood seat box within. Once, twice, three times till confident no stream of engorged rodents were going to suddenly spring forth. The Constable stepped forward and held the lantern directly above the hole cut into the wooden seat box. The better to see down into the hole dug beneath. The group holding their breath as the Constable then leant forward and stared straight through the wooden seat into the depths of the privy below. Gasping in fear as an eyeless skull

31

stared straight back up at him from a jumble of bones. Vaguely yellow in the lanterns glow.

"Mother of God." The Constable felt the earth beneath his boots shift as his breakfast rose up his throat. Held back by the iron will of the Constable's cold logic. "Don't ruin the evidence by throwing up all over. Steady yourself, man. Look again and remember all you see."

"I can't."

"Yes, you bloody well can. This is a nasty business but it's your business. This is what you signed up for. It's not all brass buttons and strolling around with your chin up. Now get on with it." Reluctantly the Constable leaned forward again and peered down into the privy. Once again the sightless sockets in the skull stared up at him. Strands of blonde hair plastered to the white of bone. Half the face gnawed clean of flesh. If I reach in, I might be able to touch it. The thought repelled the Constable who stood upright and turned about. Ushering Isac Punce out of the privy before him.

The air had never seemed so clean and clear in the Constable's lungs than it did at that moment. The sunlight finally making its way round the cottages as the morning progressed. A blessing of pure warm light. If he tried, he might forget what he'd seen but in reality he knew he never would.

"What is it? What do you see? Tell us, man, for pity's sake tell us." The fisherman shook the Constable's arm. Bringing him from his reverie back to the true horror of his situation.

"A moment if you please. I must collect myself." The Constable passed his free hand over his face as he became aware he still clutched the lantern tightly, which he slowly put down on the soil of the back yard.

"Give the man some air everyone." The same scene repeated all over again only this time it was the Constable himself, liable to suffocate from the press of the Creakers around him as the small group drew ever closer. Their frightened silence as stifling as their close presence.

"I have found those we seek." The taste of the privy seemed to be on his lips.

For a moment no one spoke. The enormity of the Constable's simple statement a blow to their collective stomachs.

"You don't mean."

"Yes. Yes, I do."

The Constable looked around at the ring of faces staring back at him. So much these faces had endured in their lives. Poverty, starvation, hardships of every kind. Now this. The absolute squalor and disrespect for the remains of their loved ones. Everything else paled into insignificance by comparison.

"The search for the missing is over. The Constable felt every eye on him as the search party hung on his words. The search for the monster responsible is now our main concern. I need everyone here to return with me and keep silent until all are assembled in the rope shed like before. Mr Punce." The fisherman blinked at the sound of his name. "I would be obliged if you would remain and stand guard until I say otherwise, this privy is not to entered or interfered with in any way by anyone unless I am present. What lies within is to be preserved at all costs."

The fisherman squared his shoulders and slammed the creaking privy door tight shut. Face a stern mask behind his beard. "Don't trouble yourself on that count." His hands closed tightly round the handle of the shovel he still carried, as he stood foursquare in front of the privy. "I'll bury any bugger who tries to interfere with our little ones again."

****

Although lunchtime beckoned and the smell of food carried from some of the cottages. Constable Hollins had little appetite for refreshment of any kind except several mugs of fresh water to wash the foul taste of the privy from his mouth. The Creakers assembled around the entrance of the rope shed to hear the dreadful news found their number swelled by two new arrivals to the hamlet. Answering the summons for their professional services the muscular, broad shouldered figure of Reverend Ball towered over his short wiry built companion, the gravedigger Eli Stone. Reverend Ball's black cassock and fine head of fair hair completely at odds with the balding, roughly dressed figure of the gravedigger. Both mature men they stood a little apart from the Creakers as they listened to Constable Hollins outline what he'd discovered, and what further action was required.

"Your arrival is most timely, Mr Stone," Constable Hollins addressed the gravedigger. "We have need of your experience but I must warn you it will be filthy work." The grave diggers surprisingly blue eyes looked up at the Constable's face from a sea of wrinkled crow's feet.

"I'm your man, sir, lead me to it and we'll get it done."

"Good man. Right everyone." Constable Hollins stared hard at the assembled crowd. "I will lead the way and no one is to hurry ahead. Remember, this is police business. I will have order while we go about recovering the bodies of the missing children. Understood?" The Constable's tone left no room for argument and a murmur of agreement swept through the Creakers. "Good, Constable Hollins turned his steps towards the track leading up to old Tom's cottage. Then let's be about it. "

With the early afternoon sun, full on their backs it took three men barely an hour to dismantle the wooden privy. Crowbarring the wooden shed like structure to pieces to lift the raised wooden box that acted as the seat to one side. The planks and box then placed out the way at one end of the small yard. Standing in a rough semi-circle about them as they worked, the assembled Creakers stood silently save for those who had lost their children. Their tears could not be contained. To the fore stood Constable Hollins and the recently arrived Reverend Ball and the gravedigger Eli Stone. Alongside the back wall of the cottages, a collection of wheel barrows and assorted handcarts stood ready to transport the children's remains the short distance from the privy, to the back door of old Tom's cottage. It being the Constable's order that the bodies be kept in the empty cottage for identification and investigative purposes.

Under the grave digger's instruction, the three men now stood three feet from the privy hole and began plying their spades and shovels to dig a ring around the actual hole. More men using wheel barrows carting the soil away to join the woodwork at the side of the yard. An hour digging had the three almost chest deep. Before they changed places with the men on the wheelbarrows, who continued deepening the ring around the privy hole until the grave digger pronounced himself satisfied, they had gone deep enough. Then began the work of digging the back out of the privy hole, by shovelling the loosened soil into the space they had created. Carefully digging until one side of the hole fell backwards across their legs.

"Right men, that's enough." The grave digger ordered the three men out of the hole and turned to Constable Hollins. "Bring up the handcarts now, sir. One for each child. I shall need another steady hand to help as I pass them up. Reverend I think now might be the time for a word or two. Might steady the crowd a bit." With a nod to the gravedigger the cassocked figure of Reverend Ball turned about to face the assembled Creakers. The warmth of the sun sending a trickle of sweat down his back. Unnoticed as he raised his hands, arms apart as if to embrace those stood before him. A seasoned veteran of funerals beyond number Reverend Ball was used to the desperate sadness of bereavement. But this was an entirely different matter and the sadness in the eyes of this impromptu congregation bought a lump to his throat. Nonetheless, the words came and the heart felt desire of Reverend Ball to ease the suffering of all present was evident in their message.

"Heavenly father, we come together in great pain and sorrow that evil has despoiled the greatest gift you bestow on the love between man and women. The gift of a child is the most precious and fulfilling blessing. That you called these little ones to your side so early in their years is trial enough for any parent to bear. Though there is consolation in the knowledge, their sacrifice has created angels to join the heavenly host. Through the theft of their mortal remains, the denial of a Christian burial and the contempt for the grief of their loved ones is an undeniable evil. I ask you heavenly father to strengthen all present with the spirit of your love and compassion that they fall not into vengeful feelings but give freely of their support for one another in this their most desperate hour. Their hearts open to the succour of your love."

The muted amens from the assembled Creakers, interspersed with sobs and cries stabbed at the heart as Reverend Ball turned to face the Constable. Arms raised hands apart. "Heavenly father. There is one amongst us who seeks to right this terrible wrong. To purge this evil from our midst. I ask you to strengthen him in all goodness and protect him as he goes about his duties."

In all his short career as a champion of law-and-order Constable Hollins had never felt the weight of his responsibilities weigh so heavy about his neck. To add to the expectation of the assembled Creakers and his superior officers. He now had the eye of the almighty watching his every move. Even Eli Stone the gravedigger was moved to comment. "Well, that should help you along nicely, Constable. Nothing like a bit of spiritual armour to ward off the sling shots off doubt and confusion." Constable Hollins favoured the gravedigger with a frosty smile.

"Thank you, Mr Stone. Now if you're ready, we have urgent matters to attend too."

With a nod of agreement, the gravedigger laid aside his jacket and pulled his rough shirt over his head to stand naked from the waist up as he adjusted a large neckerchief over his mouth and nose. Carefully he lowered himself into the exposed privy hole and slowly began the gruesome task of reclaiming the assorted bones and limbs from the soil and sludge within. Sometimes up to the elbows in slurry, as he searched every inch of the hole to make sure all the remains were accounted for. Passing up the bits and pieces of four dismembered children to his volunteer assistant. One Mrs

Potts. A middle-aged woman who acted as the local midwife, between her other fishing related duties. She it was who sorted the remains best she could to apportion four bodies onto four separate handcarts. The two of them besmirched with privy faeces and muddy soil. The assembled Creakers holding fast to the bereaved families who gave vent to terrible heart-rending shrieks as their loved ones were disinterred from their ghastly resting place. Each barrow covered with a scrap of sail cloth, wheeled inside old Tom's cottage where each set of remains was allocated a corner space in the bare room. Here the midwife went through each of the piles trying to make sure each had the requisite number of limbs. It was only then, on close inspection with most of the muck washed away from the bones that the Constable and the midwife came to the shocking conclusion almost in unison. *We only have bones with a few bits and pieces of gristle attached. Where has all their flesh gone?* Bemused the midwife kneeled on the hard floor and looked up into the face of the stunned Constable.

"Surely no rat could have eaten their bodies?" The Constable shook his head.

"The rat was big, yes, and we have reliable witnesses to prove it. Big enough to eat its way through four children and leave their bones scoured clean of flesh. Impossible. It would have been the size of a carthorse and look. The Constable held up the remnants of a thigh-bone. This bone is unmarked while this skull shows definite signs of gnawing."

"As do the other heads!" Exclaimed the midwife. "All have been chewed over and look here." The midwife rummaged amongst the skeleton piled up on the floor in front of her. Retrieving the remains of a small foot from the pile. This has also been chewed over. Yet this rib bone is as clean as a whistle without a mark on it. I tell you something's not right about all this. I don't know what to make of it but somethings just not right."

"I agree." Constable Hollins knelt down by the midwife and put his head close to hers. The rank smell of the privy clinging to her clothing making him catch his breath. "We must be careful, Mrs Potts. Please, be discreet about your findings. The families are without and I don't want to distress them any further by going off half-cocked about what might have happened." The midwife nodded in agreement, although clearly distressed and agitated she didn't want to make matters any worse.

"I'll keep my peace, don't worry. I bought all these young ones into the world and I know their mothers as friends. I'll not increase their burden. But you mark my words, young man. The midwife's tired eyes bored deep into the constables own. There's something not right about all this and others will put two and two together before long, if they haven't done so already."

Later that same afternoon Constable Hollins held court in the backyard of the cottages where all the Creakers were still gathered. His uniform stained about the knees and cuffs. His chin unshaven and his fingernails blackened by soil and faeces he still carried himself with an air of authority. "Leadership Hollins. Keep an open mind by all means but don't wander aimlessly. In the worst of circumstances people will look to you for reassurance. Remember. You are a problem solver, don't become the problem."

Unfortunately a calm exterior couldn't disguise the intensity of feeling the young Constable felt as he gave the crowd a brief overview of the day's proceedings. Most of which they had already witnessed first-hand. Then urged them to return to their homes and let the bereaved grieve in what peace they could find crammed into old Tom's cottage. "Tomorrow, the investigation would begin anew and everyone would be required to play their part. For now, everyone, himself included, needed to rest and refresh themselves for the rigours of the investigation yet to come." No one had the will to question his orders. Horror and sadness had drained the strength from all of them. Walking back to their cottages and lodgings in twos and threes, there was no conversation. No one had the will or the words. So burdened where they by the melancholy aspect of the day. A day that seemed to last a lifetime as Constable Hollins, the midwife and Reverend Ball gently ushered the last of the bereaved families through the front door of old Tom's cottage. The grim task of safeguarding the remains claimed by the gravedigger Eli Stone, who volunteered his services to keep watch while the Constable escorted the midwife back to her own small cottage.

"The dead don't bother me none. Just send me back a hot supper and a blanket and I'll bed down amongst them. Rest easy they'll be safe in my care. What's left of them. You gather your strength, Constable. You've much to do."

Gratefully the Constable joined the small party and made his way with them both along the rough track. The fading daylight a suitably drab backdrop to their tired steps. Eli Stone settling himself against the sun warmed stones of the cottage wall. His pipe bowl glowing as he inhaled the sweet-smelling smoke. Watched on as the Constable disappeared into the gloom. "I fear you'll find your body snatcher as slippery as any eel swimming in these dark waters. He murmured round the stem of the pipe, clearing his throat to spit on the rough grass between his knees. I hope you've a hook good and sharp to haul the wicked bugger in."

****

Standing at the back of the low roofed rope shed, the midwife and the Constable stared intently at the square of grey sailcloth laying on the long flat table used by the local sail maker in the manufacture and repair of the fishing boat sails. The markings on the sailcloth in question showed the full extent of the midwife's local knowledge of Bonecreake. Drawn in charcoal the squiggly lines and dabs of charcoal denoted tracks and lanes, to and from the cottages, fish, sheds and assorted out buildings as they straggled along the river bank. Old Tom's cottage highlighted. As where the locations, the children's frozen corpses had lain before the theft's had occurred. "Your absolutely sure of all this?" the Constable asked. Staring at the sailcloth as he leaned palms down over the tables.

"Yes, sir, I am." Fingers stained black by the charcoal stick the midwife didn't hesitate. "I've been midwife here most of my life and there's hardly a cottage or hovel I haven't birthed a child in hereabouts. Give or take a yard or two this is as good a map as you'll find anywhere."

"Excellent. I am truly grateful, Mrs Potts. Now. Let's identify who lives where. Those nearest old Tom's cottage first, then we'll work our way backwards to where were standing."

The charcoal stick moved in the midwife's hand like a stage magician's wand as initials appeared next to the cottages. Until all were accounted for, occupied and empty alike, Constable Hollins listening intently as the midwife spoke each name aloud, "Nearest family to old Tom's is the Hendon's, next to them the shean's . Both those places are just on the bend of the track leading down to the river and behind them, backing onto the open land, the Jiller's."

"Open land," inquired the Constable.

"Land left," be answered the midwife. It's too stony to be much use for farming and riddled with pot holes, bogs and hollows. You'd like as not break your leg trying to walk over it. No one lives past that point where Maudy Jillers old place sits."

"I see." The Constable reflected on the midwife's words as he urged her to carry on. "The initials gradually moving down the cloth to the small harbour where they ended."

"That's your lot, sir. The midwife laid the charcoal pencil aside and rubbed her stained fingers through a handful of frayed rope to wipe of the excess. Make of it what you will but there's Bonecreak and the Creakers all accounted for."

Constable Hollins stood silently for a moment before questioning the midwife about the distance between the various cottages and old Tom's cottage. Paying particular attention to the time it would take to walk between the different areas where the children died and where there remains had been found. The midwife picked up her charcoal once again and pencilled in some rough figures. Five minutes to this cottage, ten to the next and so on.

"Now how much does a small child weigh, do you think? In particular the missing children?"

The midwife frowned and pursed her lips before replying. "Hmm. There's been little enough food to go round these last three months, so it's been empty bellies all around. To be honest I don't think anybody in Bonecreakes had a full stomach in recent memory. So the bodies wouldn't have been very heavy to carry."

"Really?" The Constable turned slightly and stood upright to face the midwife. I never realised things could be so bad. Some items were hard to come by certainly but food was always plentiful in town. Why didn't someone brave the elements to secure fresh supplies?"

"Money, sir. Moneys at the root of it. There's little enough at the best of times and in the winter months there's likely none at all. You can't buy food with fresh air and no shop keeper will give a Creaker credit. Knowing the hand to mouth life we live and I can't say I blame them. Now, sir." The midwife dusted the charcoal from her fingers once more. "If you've all you need I have other duties to attend to."

Constable Hollins smiled through the stubble of a three-day beard and walked behind the midwife as she weaved her way through the equipment stored hap hazardly in the rope shed. The pair of them breaking step as the midwife looked about her to check they were all alone as they approached the open entrance. "There is one other matter, sir." Constable Hollins leaned closer to the midwife. "I'm afraid it's kept me up half the night thinking about it. But I reckon them bones we dug up yesterday had been boiled to strip the flesh of them. In fact I'm sure of it." The Constable stood silently as the midwife looked about her again. The enormity of what she was suggesting so unnerving as to heighten her fear of other ears hearing her speak. "God forgive me for saying such a thing, sir but it's all I can think of that would leave them bones so clean." With that, the midwife gathered her skirts and walked briskly through the entrance, and out into the daylight of another fine spring day. Eager to leave the fear of her suspicions for the dishevelled constable to deal with.

Watching her walk away, Constable Hollins rubbed his grimy hands over his fledgling beard. Speaking softly through his fingers as the smell of charcoal and canvas filled his nostrils. "It may be little consolation to you, Madam, but I am absolutely certain someone boiled those bones. It's who, where and why I am not certain about?"

****

The rest of that day Constable Hollins walked the rough tracks joining the straggle of Bonecreake's homes and businesses together. The charcoal lines on the sailcloth, fresh in his memory as he walked hands behind his back. Deep in thought as the early morning sunshine gave way to cloud filled skies overhead. Here and there, he stopped and considered his surroundings in detail. Measuring distances and positions in his head as his boots crunched on the drying track beneath his tread. Faces and names like a jigsaw puzzle flitting across his thoughts as he strove to piece together all the information he had gathered since his arrival. He had a motive clear in his head now but was still grappling with the who and the how of it as the steadily rising track gave way to the stone littered open land which bought him to a standstill. "I understand what you mean," murmured Constable Hollins through dry lips. The midwife's description of the stone strewn fields stretching out in front of him fresh in his mind. "Full of holes and humps and littered with grey-brown stones of every shape and size. An area of land at odds with its

44

surrounding flat, even neighbours. Useless for farming," the midwife had said. Yet it would seem a place of great enjoyment for at least two little figures, dodging nimble footed from outcrop to outcrop. One hiding from the other as they played. Laughter faint yet discernible on the breeze.

Well, I never mused the constable. His spirits lifted by the sight and sound of children at play. *I never thought to hear laughter in such melancholy surroundings. At least the troubles of the adults has spared these little ones. They seem full of life. A shame the rest of the little Creakers are not so joyous.* The smile on the constable's face froze as he thought of the rest of the children, he'd come across in Bonecreake. Pale, half-starved creatures. Skin and bone lot of them clinging close to their mother's skirts fearful of being spirited away when they should have been full of energy and mischief.

"My God." Constable Hollins sank to his knees as the full horror of his thoughts overwhelmed him. The two children immersed in their own enjoyment drawing closer to the kneeling figure watching their every move. His dusty blue uniform blending in harmoniously with the cloud-filled skies and the bare branches of the scattered scrub and bushes littering the slightly rising ground. Their laughter suddenly overlaid with another high-pitched voice. A rattling shout that bought both the children up smartly to attention. A voice of command that brooked no argument. "Girls."

Constable Hollins watched as both the ragged figures hurried off down the slope towards a ramshackle stone cottage, some 200 yards from where he knelt. Racing each other to obey the gaunt scarecrow like figure who stood arms crossed in the small fenced in cottage garden. Even if he hadn't turned to watch the girls run home Constable Hollins would have recognised that reedy rattling voice. Maudy Jiller as I live and breathe. A very angry Maudy Jiller by the sound of it as the rattling voice carried over the open land. "Get in here, you stupid little buggers. Didn't I tell you both to stay indoors till I got back?" The girls obviously knew better than to provoke their mothers temper further and stood silently as harsh words rained down over them.

"Blast your eyes, I should thrash you both. What if you'd been seen?" The last the constable heard as the three of them disappearing round the side of the cottage, to where he supposed the door to be. The harsh words confirming his worst fears.

Some 20 minutes later as he walked back along the top of the river bank to the rope store, which had become his unofficial base of operations. Constable Hollins, who now felt he knew the why and the who of the case, found himself face to face with the how of the missing children's disappearance. Once again it was so obvious to those who knew of the existence of such things but to an outsider like himself the basket sledges where a complete mystery. Likely to have remained so if the small fishing boat had not been unloading her catch at the river's edge. Fresh caught shellfish filling square wicker baskets, sat two aside each other on a small sledge some two feet wide by three feet long. Either end curved upwards to prevent the sledge digging into the uneven bank and to stop the small baskets slipping off as a rope handle at either end of the sledge was tied to longer ropes. One leading to the boat, the other up to the top of the sloping riverbank. A method unchanged for years that saw two stout women pull the full baskets up the bank. Lift them off the sledge onto their flat handcarts. While the fishermen pulled the empty sledge back down the bank as one of the women paid out her end of the rope to keep the sledge straight. The whole process repeated time and again, until all the baskets where piled high on the handcarts. The basket sledge left atop the riverbank ready for the next boat to unload.

Humming contentedly Constable Hollins stopped and took note of the lightweight construction of the sledge as he followed the two women along the track atop the riverbank. Making a mental note here and there as he strolled by first one location where a child had disappeared, then another. Before turning off the bank to walk along a narrow alleyway between several properties, where another child had disappeared, before reaching the spot where the final child had gone missing. All within a short walk of the river bank. The jigsaw puzzle of recent events falling into place piece by piece, as he reached the rope shed and passed the word for Isac Punce to join him.

"I require a few oddments of information about the river and tides of the estuary," he explained to the sallow faced young boy, who repeated the constable's words back to him before scurrying off to find the burly fisherman. His business known by all before he had gone a hundred yards.

An hour later Isac Punce joined Constable Hollins at the rear of the rope shed. Alone the two men conferred. Thick as thieves in the shadows. Constable Hollins speaking softly to guard against eavesdroppers. Shock writ large on the fisherman's face as he turned about and left the constable staring down at the sail cloth map of Bonecreake. The charcoal lines and initials reinforcing his belief that he had the body snatcher firmly in his sights. Tomorrow will see the end of this sordid affair.

"Are you sure of your ground, Hollins?"

"I am, sir."

"Then go to man and let's have an end to this sorry business."

The night before the arrest seemed to last way beyond the allotted hours of darkness and Constable Hollins slept little as he lay abed. Much still remained to be done but nothing could be done before daybreak. The normal business of Bonecreake would see most of the Creakers up and about before first light to catch the early tide. Those remaining ashore would be preparing for the catch to be landed and dealing with the general business of the day. Tomorrow, however, the bodies of the deceased, all 27 of them, where due to be laid to rest in Bonecreake's small desolate cemetery with all the evidence gathered and the warming weather thawing the frozen bodies. There was no reason to delay proceedings any longer, so the normal business of the day would be put aside for a day of mourning and good byes. With all the Creakers paying their last respects. Among them, hiding in plain sight the body snatcher would no doubt be in attendance. Constable Hollins hands twitched and clenched into fists under the coarse blankets. Chafing at the delay now an arrest was imminent. "You won't be hiding much longer, you heartless bastard. As God's, my witness, I'll have you behind bars before another day passes. Constable Hollins let out an exasperated sigh that chased the shadows round the darkened room. That's if this night ever ends."

****

Reverend Ball stood solemnly to the side as Eli Stone the gravedigger, assisted by four men of Bonecreake. Apportioned each body to its allotted grave. Gently lowering them into their freshly dug resting place, their every move watched by the assembled Creakers, lining the outside of the low-stone wall that defined the cemetery from the surrounding expanse of coarse grass meadow. Three deep in places, a palpable wave of sadness hung over their tear-streaked faces. The remains of the four stolen children stitched into sailcloth sacks as opposed to sailcloth shrouds. Occasioning many sobs and mournful cries of anguish, as they were carried into the small cemetery. The final resting place for youth so cruelly used.

Watching on Constable Hollins kept a respectful silence as Reverend Ball stepped forward and called the mourners to order. There being so many deceased, individual funerals had given way to a collective service, that would see all the deceased Creakers laid to rest in their individual graves at the same time. That being the case and with such a crowd assembled. Reverend Ball stood up on a small dais of sturdy wooden fish crates. Though his robes flapped around his ankle and the pages of his bible ruffled in the ever-present onshore breeze. All present could now hear him and see his actions clearly.

"We are gathered here today to give thanks for the lives of our loved ones." Reverend Ball's voice carried above the soft moan of the breeze. As he listed one by one the names of the deceased. Making no distinction between those stolen and those not. "Now they are gone from of us to be at peace in eternal sleep where no harm may befall them."

With the ease of many years practice. Reverend Ball progressed smoothly through the service. Whilst Constable Hollins bided his time. One eye on the crowd, the other scanning the rough track behind the assembled mourners that wound its way from Bonecreake to the cemetery. Overhead disturbed from their normal perches on the small head stones and wooden crosses of Bonecreake's departed. Scavenging seagulls formed a melancholy choir with their forlorn calls. So cruel on the ear that many thought their loved ones cried a final heart-rending goodbye from the grave.

Unmoved by such fanciful thoughts Constable Hollins watched and waited. Much as he had when first he addressed the assembled Creakers in the shadowy confines of the rope shed. No doubt, he reflected ruefully, the body snatcher had hung on his every word. Much as the assembled mourners now hung on every word. Some wishing the moment to last forever. Distraught at the finality of losing their loved ones to a cold unfeeling grave. Others wishing the day over and done with. Unsettled in the presence of such overwhelming sadness.

"Almighty God, as you once called these brothers and sisters into this life."

Reverend Ball began the final few sentences of the funeral service, just as a small group of people appeared around the bend in the track behind the assembled mourners.

"So now you have called them into life everlasting. We therefore commit their bodies to the ground. Their final resting place. Earth to earth, ashes to ashes, dust to dust."

The small group held back as the final words of the service carried on the wind towards them.

"We faithfully give them over to your blessed care. Reverend Ball closed the bible in his cold hands with a soft snap of the leather cover as he and the crowd intoned the final word to complete the service. A ragged and tear filled amen."

Waiting just a moment longer until Reverend Ball stepped down from his fish crate dais and moved aside. Constable Hollins made his move. Hopping nimbly up on the same fish crate's and clapping his hands loudly. Shock briefly replacing the sadness in the Creaker's eyes at the constable's unseemly behaviour.

"Ladies and Gentlemen. If I may have your attention." Every face looked back at his own. A silence descending on the small cemetery as the breeze suddenly dropped and the sea gulls fell silent in anticipation.

"Ladies and Gentlemen, please forgive what must seem an inappropriate intrusion into your grief but I have police business to attend to that will not wait a moment longer. Indeed to give you all peace of mind to grieve your loved one's it must not wait." Over the heads of the crowd constable Hollins watched the small group on the track draw nearer.

"I told you when I started to investigate the disappearance of your children that I suspected one of your own was responsible. Sadly. I am now in a position to confirm my initial suspicions were correct and that the person responsible is a Creaker. Born and raised, standing without shame here amongst you today."

The small group, two men and two children drew nearer yet.

Shock, grief, growing anger. The faces of the mourning Creakers exhibited every emotion possible as many amongst them stood open mouthed in surprise.

"Who came the cry? Taken up by several others as the crowd pressed hard against the low cemetery wall. Who is it? You have proof demanded another?"

Constable Hollins raised his arms waist high and went through his by now familiar routine of asking for calm. Hands palm down patting the air in front of him.

"Calm yourselves, all of you. Yes, sadly, I have a proof."

Here Constable Hollins beckoned the small group standing unnoticed behind the main body of the crowd.

"Make way there. Please, come forward, Sergeant Crane."

The bemused Creakers looked about them in surprise as they stood aside to allow the group access to the cemetery where they stood before Constable Hollins. Two well-built men, one wearing a blue brass-buttoned uniform identical to the constables save for three white chevrons on the upper arms, the other man none other than the familiar figure of Isac Punce the fisherman. The two young girls between them drawing back the heavy woollen shawls covering their heads to stand confused and nervous.

"Thank you, sergeant, I..."

A rattling scream cut off the constable's words as the gaunt figure of Maudy Jiller pushed her way to the front of the crowd and jumped over the low wall in a flurry of ragged skirts. "My girls," she shouted at the top of her lungs. "My babies." Her cries answered immediately by the two young girls Constable Hollins had observed playing hide and seek amongst the stone littered empty land the day before.

"Stay where you are, Mrs Jiller."

Constable Hollins's deep voice raised in a shout, halted Maudy Jiller mid stride, halfway between her crying children and the bemused crowd of Creakers.

"I have business with you, Mrs Jiller." Constable Hollins stared down at the ragged woman in front of him from his perch on the fish crate's. His stare met with glacial coldness by the sunken eyes of Maudy Jiller.

"I thought long and hard about the strange goings on here in Bonecreake, Mrs Jiller." Constable Hollins's voice held everyone in its grip as he spoke, "I kept asking myself the same question. Why would anyone steal the dead? What value did they have? What use could they be? I couldn't fathom it until I watched your daughters at play. Running happy and free of worry."

"What of it? Children play all the time. It's no business of yours." Maudy Jiller's jaw thrust forward like a bulldog picking a fight, her entire body shook as she shouted back at the blue uniformed constable.

"Oh, it's my business, all right? And that makes it police business, Mrs Jiller. You see I have watched everyone going about their business these last few days and one thing stuck out in my mind."

The crowd hung on every word and craned their necks the better to watch the confrontation between the Constable and the fishwife.

"Mrs Jiller, the thing that struck me when I watched your daughters at play was that I hadn't seen or heard any of the other children in Bonecreake at play."

"Well," the rattling voice demanded. "What of it?"

"What of it indeed, Mrs Jiller?" Constable Hollins fired Maudy Jiller's harsh words straight back at her. "The what off it is that the children of Bonecreake are a starving malnourished lot without the strength or enthusiasm to muster a game of any sort between them. Mired down in grief. Held close to their mother's skirts for fear of being stolen away. They are as miserable a bunch of waifs as you could hope to find. Skin and bones the lot of them. Kept behind closed doors despite winter giving way to spring. The children of Bonecreake are as near to invisible as it's possible for children to be."

"And that's a crime, is it? Maudy Jiller's retorted. Other people's children are not running round in the sunshine, so my daughters should be denied this simple, pleasure."

"No, Mrs Jiller." The Constables measured tones cut through the contemptuous note in the fishwife's rattling voice. "Your daughters at play is not a crime but where they got the strength and enthusiasm to play in such a carefree way is. I put it to you, Mrs Jiller, that despite your malnourished appearance, your daughters appear to be a picture of good health. Well-fed and rosy cheeked as you would expect thriving youngsters to be."

The shrill laughter that came from somewhere deep inside the bones of Maudy Jillers ribcage set the ear on edge. Shrill, high-pitched. It had an unnerving quality that spoke of madness in dark lonely places.

"You fool. You know nothing of being a mother yet you stand there on them fish crates like a preacher in his pulpit. Solemnising about well-fed children like you have a family of your own to feed and clothe. Well, boy," she screeched sarcastically. Do you have children? Do you have a wife?"

"No, I have neither," responded Constable Hollins calmly.

"Neither." The word seemed to hang in the air before the breeze whipped it away over the Creaker's heads. "You have neither, yet in your ignorance you come up with some cock

54

and bull nonsense about children at play being sinful and a crime against children whose parents keep them close. The ragged figure wheezed through her nose in a snort of derision. You don't know what it is to be a mother. If you ask me, you know nothing about anything. Except shining the buttons on your blue suit and strutting round like a preening peacock. It's a mother's way to feed her young first you young fool. Even if it means no share for her. Look around you. Here a bony arm raised from the folds of her rags and waved at the crowd. There's not a mother here who hasn't gone without to feed her children. If it's a mothers lot to starve so they might live then so be it. A mother always feeds her children first and keeps them as well as she can."

Murmurs of agreement came from the crowd as Maudy Jiller laid into Constable Hollins. Her words hitting a chord within many of the mothers present.

"As you say, Mrs Jiller." Constable Hollins held the fishwife's stare with unblinking eyes. "It's what you fed your children with that concerns me?"

The sudden intake of breath from the crowd sounded like a set of fireside bellows drawing air into its leather lungs as a dreadful realisation began to take hold.

"Well, Mrs Jiller. Will you tell us all what you fed your children on over and above the dried fish and provisions you stored away during the summer?"

"No. you have no voice."

Maudy Jiller's sunken eyes darted this way and that. Bony fingers clenching into tight fists.

"Well, let me tell you and put an end to this deceitful charade." Constable Hollnis paused, breathed deeply and spoke calmly. You fed your own children on the flesh of your

55

neighbour's dead children. Whose bodies you stole and dismembered in old Tom's cabin. You, Maudy Jiller, denied yourself food to keep up the appearance of starvation, whilst feeding your daughters on soups and stews made from the meat and boiled bones of the deceased. You. Maudy Jiller turned your unknowing innocent daughters into cannibals."

"I did not and you can't prove anything of the sort." The ragged fishwife shook with anger. Her gaunt face flushed brick red.

Constable Hollins allowed himself a grim smile as he turned slightly and looked at the two young girls between Sergeant Crane and Isac Punce.

"I don't need to prove anything, Mrs Jiller. Your well-fed daughters are proof enough. Is that not so, Sergeant Crane?"

"It is, Constable." Sergeant Crane glanced down at the daughter nearest to him as he held her hand. Well-fed and talkative in their innocence your daughters have told all with Mr Punce and myself as witnesses to their words."

For a moment the small cemetery seemed frozen in time. Statue like no one moved a muscle until one of the two girls. As if suddenly realising every eye was on her, cried out and burst into tears. The sound loud against the silence.

"Get your filthy hands off my babies." Maudy Jiller was a mother's anger incarnate as she turned about and lunged at the two men. Each holding tight the hand of one of her two daughters as the enraged mother closed the space between her children and herself. "I'll kill you," she screamed in her curious rattling way. A slim bladed, filleting knife appearing from the folds of her clothing. Razor sharp and deadly as the woman wielding it. "I'll kill you both, you interfering bastards."

With that Maudy Jiller grabbed the front of her nearest daughter's jacket and tried to wrestle her free while she slashed at the face of Sergeant Crane. The thin knife blade glinting as it swung through the air. The children's frightened screams exciting the sea gulls into a high-pitched response, filling the sky with cries of fear and anger as the violent confrontation unfolded before them.

"Maudy," the familiar voice of Isac Punce shouted above the uproar as he released his grip on the young girl in his charge. Reaching out to try and restrain the enraged mother. "Maudy, stop this madness." His cries joined by a scream of pain, as the knife blade sliced open the sleeve of Sergeant Crane's police tunic, opening a long wound through the flesh of his forearm down into the palm of his hand. A torrent of blood spraying from beneath the torn clothing. The shock loosening the stricken sergeant's grip on the child's hand, she fell forward as Maudy Jiller tugged hard at her jacket. Her released daughter landing at her feet. Maudy Jiller immediately closed with Isac Punce. Face stretched into a mask of hatred as the knife blade flashed across the fisherman's face and grazed his chin, cutting three inches of his beard. "Enough of this" bellowed Isac Punce. Wrapping his arms around Maudy Jillers bony waist, trapping both her arms against her sides as he lifted her off her feet. "You traitorous bastard Isac Punce. The fisherman felt the hot breath of hatred on his part shaved face as Maudy Jiller wriggled like a hooked fish in his encircling grasp. I'll do for you yet". With both her daughters clinging to her skirts and crying at the top of their voices in fear. Maudy Jiller arched her neck muscles and head butted Isac Punce straight in the mouth. Once, twice, three times before she clamped her teeth around his nose and bit down as hard as she could. The battered and dazed fisherman swaying like tall grass in a breeze, shouted out as Maudy Jiller's teeth bit down through flesh and cartilage. The indescribable pain causing him to stagger and loosen his grip. Vainly trying to push the skeletal figure away, as her teeth ground together on the flesh of his nose. Blood blowing from her biting mouth in frothy bubbles that blew away in the breeze to splash red droplets against Reverend Ball's white robes. The knife, someone screamed from the crowd. The knife. The knife free again of any restraint had lost its shine as Sergeant Cranes blood dried on the blade, but retained all its lethal sharpness as Maudy Jiller. Still biting the face of Isac Punce lifted her arm to strike the fisherman, what would surely have been a lethal blow. Had not Constable Hollins jumped off the raised fish crate's and grabbed Maudy Jiller's stick thin arm before the knife could strike home. His haste causing him to collide forcibly with Maudy Jiller's two daughters. The collision pushing both girls hard into Maudy Jiller's lower back, just as Isac Punce lost his footing and fell backwards into one of the freshly dug graves. Taking the wrestling screaming woman, her two daughters and Constable Hollins with him to land in a struggling tangle of bloodied arms and legs atop the shroud wrapped corpse, lying in what should have been peaceful repose.

The stunned Creakers were rooted to the spot. So quickly had the wild events unfolded in front of them they were frozen into immobility. Sergeant Crane to his credit had ripped off his tunic and stood in his shirtsleeves. Torn arm bent at the elbow, his free hand squeezing the wound closed best he could to staunch the flow of blood, that had soaked his clothing red. He at least had the presence of mind to yell aloud for assistance as the wrestling match inside the confines of the grave erupted in a piercing scream that was the undoing of several present, who fainted away to lie at the feet of their neighbours.

"Help him, for god's sake help him. Get that bloody knife before she does murder."

Surprisingly the first to react was Reverend Ball who snatched up the gravedigger's spade and hurried around the open graves to peer down into the melee within. Gauging his moment perfectly he bought the flat steel of the spade down in a short double handed swing. Striking Maudy Jiller with all his might right across the top of her head. The hollow thud as steel met flesh sounding across the cemetery as loud as a pistol shot. The hate filled bloodied face of Maudy Jiller, twisting round to stare at this new attacker living long in Reverend Ball's memory, as Eli Stone dropped smartly to his knees by the graveside, and plucked the deadly knife from the stunned woman's loosened grip.

"Grab her, quickly," now yelled Sergeant Crane. "Move yourselves blast you."

The spell was broken. The Creakers as one clambered over the low wall and within minutes, Maudy Jiller's unconscious body lay on the piled earth of the grave from whence she had been lifted. One of her two daughters shaking uncontrollably kneeled by her side. Constable Hollins sporting a black eye and cuts and scratches to his neck, climbed free of the confining grave under his own steam. Shaken but otherwise in good order. Not so, Isac Punce. The burly fisherman was in a bad way. His mouth, nose and one eye bloodied and badly torn about. He had suffered a terrible beating and was barely conscious as he slumped against the low stone wall. The horror associated with the scream prior to Reverend Ball's intervention now became clear, as the body of Maudy Jillers second daughter was lifted from the grave. By a strange trick of fate she had ended up underneath everyone as Isac Punce had fallen backwards. Her childish bones no match for the weight piled upon them had bent and twisted until her head, driven down into the unyielding body of the corpse beneath, rolled sideways beyond the limit of natural movement. Her neck breaking under the immense strain. Now, limp as a rag doll, her limbs hung loose as Eli Stone lifted her lifeless body from the depths of the grave. The gravedigger's face as hard as the stone in his surname as he mastered his own emotions.

"This is a bad business, Hollins. Sergeant Crane, ashen-faced and bloodied in his shirt sleeves looked near to collapse himself as he spoke with his black eyed junior. A bad business."

"I agree sergeant but I never envisaged any of this when I laid my plans. I sought only to expose Maudy Jiller as the body snatcher. Then get her in irons and explain my case later when she was safely under lock and key. I knew her to be a bitter cantankerous woman but I never dreamt she was capable of such extreme violence."

Despite his own pain Sergeant Crane looked on his young constable with sympathy and managed a weak smile. "You have much to learn about women and their ways, Hollins. Especially when a mother feels her children threatened or at risk of harm. Had I but known your plan in detail. I would have advised against it and nabbed our culprit when she was alone in her property. Sergeant Crane shook with cold and shock as Constable Hollins retrieved his blood-stained tunic from the ground, and draped it round the wounded man's shoulders. But it's done now so we'd best get ourselves organised before the crowd give her a taste of their own rough justice."

With a curt nod to his stricken Sergeant. Constable Hollins sprang into life. Still unconscious. Maudy Jiller was bound hand and foot and thrown roughly onto one of the flat-bodied hand carts used earlier to transport the deceased Creakers to the cemetery. Reverend Ball standing watch over her to prevent her escape or murder as the occasion demanded. With the help of his fellow Creakers, the much-bloodied Isac Punce was helped onto another cart and slowly wheeled down the track leading back to Bonecreake. Sergeant Crane following on behind in likewise fashion. Mrs Potts, the midwife, hurrying ahead to boil water and prepare her rudimentary medical equipment to render what first aid and comfort she could for the injured men. Mindful of his responsibilities to the grieving families still gathered round the cemetery. Eli Stone was already at work back filling the open graves and positioning small wooden markers to indicate who lay where. There being no further reason to linger around the windswept cemetery most of the Creakers. Bemused though they were by recent events, slowly followed Constable Hollins and Reverend Ball as two of their own manhandled the wooden handcart and its unconscious cargo down the rough track back to Bonecreake. The cries of the wheeling gulls overhead spurring them on their way as the breeze stiffened at their backs.

****

The position of the heavy wooden desk reflected the rank of the two men. Constable Hollins, standing on one side, hands behind his back, freshly shaved, uniform pressed, buttons polished. Seated on the other side his senior officer. Captain Ramsey Blades. A short, slightly built ex-cavalry officer sitting upright and alert, showing no sign of benign old age despite being well into his sixties. A lifetime of military service under his highly polished belt. The hand written report detailing the case of the missing children of Bonecreake and the part played in their disappearance by Maudy Jiller lay open on the desk before him. A report Captain Blades had studied with a growing sense of unease.

"The stuff of nightmares, Constable."

"Indeed, sir." Constable Hollins kept his answer neutral.

"You are no doubt aware of the level of public interest in this case."

"I am, sir. The newspapers are already full of it."

"Yes." Captain Blades tapped the report with his finger. Thin lips pursed in disapproval. "I have read some of the more lurid headlines but this is what matters, Constable. This report is what the judiciary will rely on when formulating the case against Maudy Jiller. That and your testimony in court when the case comes to trial." The braided epaulettes on the senior officer's uniform glinted as he leaned forward. Brightness in an otherwise functional room.

"You have done well, Hollins. Very well indeed to bring this woman to book for her crimes. Lesser men would have foundered given the difficult circumstances. You have a keen mind, Constable. Common sense and sound reasoning have served you well despite your relative inexperience in the field."

"Thank you, sir."

Despite himself Constable Hollins couldn't stop a mixture of embarrassment and relief flooding through him as he relaxed slightly. The memory of Sergeant Crane, bloodied and faint with pain. Isac Punce beaten and disfigured. The flopping loose limbs of Maudy Jiller's dead daughter. The complete mess he'd made of the actual arrest had cost him sleep despite the best efforts of others to reassure him.

"It's done, Hollins," Sergeant Crane had spoken through gritted teeth as Mrs Potts the midwife cleaned and stitched his wounded arm. "It's done and can't be undone and there's no profit in agonising over other people's pain. Naivety betrayed you but you've gained experience and there's no substitute for experience. Knowing what you know now, you won't make the same mistakes again."

"No, Sergeant, I certainly will not."

The creak of the chair legs dragging across the floorboards as Captain Blades pushed himself away from the desk. Made Constable Hollins flinch at the reminder of creaking nails forced from woodwork during the demolition of old Tom's privy. The smell and taste of faeces and wet soil hanging in his memory.

"You don't forget. Much as you might want, you don't. That's the nature of the job we do, Hollins. Grubbing round in honesty's gutter."

"How do you deal with it, Sergeant? You must have seen plenty to unsettle you."

"Let it have its moment, Hollins. Then carry on about your duties. Remember, you have a future. Memories do not."

"Well, Constable."

Standing upright Captain Blades only came up to Constable Hollins's shoulder but the diminutive figure had an undeniable presence. The hand offered across the desk in a congratulatory handshake, firm and strong, had held other men's lives in its grip.

"It is within my authority to gauge the suitability of my officers for the duties I order them to undertake. Sharp eyes held the constable like a moth pinned to a board. I had high hopes of you when you joined the force Hollins. I am pleased to see my hopes become reality. Keep up the good work. Once this affair is settled and the case closed. We shall speak again. I have a role in mind better suited to your investigative talents than routine police work."

"Yes, sir, thank you, sir."

"Thank you, Constable." The handshake and the meeting were over. That will be all.

****

In the subsequent two weeks between her arrest and trial, little was seen or heard of Maudy Jiller as she languished in the small-town jail. A gloomy stone-built turreted building containing ten cells with solid doors and small slit windows set high up in the stonework. Her surroundings and circumstances as hard and indifferent as they could be from being her own mistress with the freedom to do as she pleased. Not that Maudy Jiller seemed to know what was going on around her half the time. The warden charged with her welfare reported the waning health of his celebrity prisoner to his senior officers. "Who, alarmed at her daily decline, summoned a doctor to examine the prisoner languishing in cell five? Her overall welfare of secondary importance to keeping her alive for her trial and the harsh justice which was expected to follow. The doctor's report was not encouraging."

"She dying, that's beyond doubt. She takes little food and less water. The blow to her head has damaged her senses and the death of one daughter and the incarceration of the other in an asylum for the insane, has robbed her of all vitality. It is my professional opinion gentlemen that the prisoner has given up the will to live. Her injuries and self-starvation can be treated by care, time and force feeding but her desire to embrace death cannot be altered by any means at my disposal. I respectfully suggest that justice be served at its earliest convenience or your prisoner will die and justice will be denied."

Within an hour of the doctor's departure a hastily convened meeting within the oak panelled chambers of Sir William Blackford took place. The circuit judge who would preside over proceedings at Maudy Jiller's trial, listened intently as the doctor's report was repeated. Mr Quiller. The judge's clerk. Who shuffled the dates in the court diary and between Judge, clerk and representatives of prison and police. A date was decided upon. The trial of Maudy Jiller was set to commence in two days' time.

It seemed within moments of the ink drying on the pages of Judge Blackford's diary, the whole world knew of the trial date. The court buildings containing the ten cells, and adjoining police station, quietly busy at the best of times, became a hive of bustling activity in preparation for what was fast turning into the event of the judicial year. Not that the reason for all the excitement was interested. Maudy Jiller had demons of her own to wrestle with and they cared little for the affairs of men.

"You're a monster, Maudy Jiller. The sing song voice sneaked through the bruises in her brain. A curse, a blasphemy, a pestilence. You're evil, Maudy Jiller. Oh, but you led them all a merry dance until they hunted you down. Now you'll do a jig for all to see when the hangman hangs you on his gallows tree. You're a murderer, Maudy Jiller. A deceiving mean-hearted whore of a murderer. The laughter rattled in the bony chest and chased round her nerves like her daughters playing in the lost lands under Constable Hollins's watchful eyes. One daughter dead, the other driven insane. Oh, Maudy sweet Maudy, what have you done to cause your loved ones such pain? Pray tell us sweet Maudy with a voice that rattles like the rain. Tell us how you stole and killed and caused your neighbours so much pain?"

Lips thin, blue and bloodless moved in Maudy Jiller's gaunt face and one bloodshot eye opened blinking in the near darkness of the unlit cell.

"I'll tell," she whispered. "I'll tell the whole world." Laughter born in misery spilled out of her parched throat as she crawled across the cold stone floor of the cell. Using both sides of one corner, easing herself slowly, hand over hand to stand tremblingly upright. Her bony shoulders pressed into the rough stone. Palms flat against the walls to support her weight. Bare feet planted firmly to force her fleshless hips back into the angle of the adjoining walls.

"Pray tell us sweet Maudy. Pray tell us again. How you caused all your loved ones never ending pain?"

The song died in her senses as the other bloodied eye opened and an agonised scream that shook the warden on duty to his core echoed from her rattling chest. Chasing itself around the bare stone walls of the uncaring cell.

"She's awake, your honour."

"Eh. What's that?"

"The prisoner Jiller, your honour. Awake and demanding food and water."

"So, stirred herself, has she? Well, all to the good, Mr Quiller. We shall see what she has to say for herself and proceed accordingly."

"Quite so, your honour. Quite so."

The extent to which Maudy Jiller's apparent recovery from her injuries, galvanised those with an interest in the proceedings could not be understated. Come the day of the trial there was mayhem in the street outside the court building. Where a large crowd had assembled in the hope of a seat in the small public gallery, overlooking the well of the court. This occasioned much pushing and shoving, particularly amongst the members of the press covering the trial for their respective publications. Freely used, elbows became the weapon of choice and more than one set of ribs was bruised before the police constables on duty restored order of sorts. The diminutive figure of Captain Blades coming to his men's aid astride a magnificent black mare. Forcing through the crowd and driving them back with a skilful display of crowd control at close quarters.

"Back damn you, back. Keep order there." The horse's bulk driving a wedge between the entrance doors to the court and the mob of would-be spectators.

Those already within the court proper. Clerks, ushers and other such officers of the court could hear the fearful racket from without but true to their calling maintained a sober detached air as they went about their duties. Billy Blackheart. As Judge William Blackford was referred to by the wags in the legal trade was not a man to be trifled with. Arthritic and irritated by gnawing pains in his joints, his temper was uneven at the best of times. Any unseemly displays in his court by a court official. Would see said official seeking opportunities elsewhere. With that chastening thought in mind, the court officials maintained a decorous silence.

Seated on a hard wooden chair at the side of the court near the empty bench from which his honour Judge Blackford would shortly open proceedings. Constable Hollins sat in quiet contemplation, writing up his report from his notes had been simple enough. Facts presented in chronological order with a start, beginning and end. Hardly a bestseller but exactly what was required. It was reading between the neat lines of his own hand writing that gave Constable Hollins pause for thought. The investigative talents Captain Blades was keen to exploit demanded answers, knowing what Maudy Jiller had done and why she did it was all very well but could the crime have been prevented in the first place? A thorny issue that had occasioned many social commentators of the day to speculate, that rather than perpetrator. Maudy Jiller was in fact a victim, who should be supported rather than condemned. Indeed there was great sympathy among many social reformers demanding leniency for a mother driven by circumstances beyond her control, to such desperate measures, she had resorted to cannibalism to feed her starving children. Arguments that raged back and forth across the pages of the broadsheets, further heightening interest in the case.

"The whole countries in a ferment Hollins like fighting dogs, the do gooders and punishers are at each other's throats.

All of which cut little ice with the honourable Judge Blackford. His court crammed to the rafters with quality and commoner alike. All eager as excitable schoolchildren to lay eyes on the monster of the marshes. A lurid headline that struck a chord and excited much speculation as to the physical makeup of the prisoner. "Teeth like razors I heard, fingernails like claws to tear the flesh from the bones, drinks the blood before she boils them, you know."

"Children eaten alive."

The paperboys bawling the latest from their roadside pitches, could hardly keep pace with demand as an excitable public hungered for more. Those lucky enough to have the strongest elbows, positively shaking with excitement when the court doors closed and the court usher rose to open proceedings.

"All rise."

The court was on its feet in an instant.

For the excitable crowd the first sight of Judge Blackford set the tone for the morbid thrill seeking to come. A man in his 50th year, tall and well-made through the chest and shoulders. The constant nagging pain of arthritis made his impressive stature a curse for his agitated lower joints to bear. His passage up the four steps to his raised seat beneath the royal crest carved into the woodwork of the polished panelling lining the court was a personal nightmare. Beneath his black robes of office, his ankles, knees and hips grated bone on bone. Groaning in protest. Consequently the near permanent scowl on the judges lined-face deepened with every step. By the time he took his seat, he resembled nothing more than a stiff legged crow. Stalking across the court like a harbinger of doom. His humour not helped in the slightest by the packed public gallery, nudging each other and talking to their fellows in loud stage whispers.

"Silence."

Judge Blackford's voice hit the woodwork of the building and rebounded back across the open spaces within. Boxing the ears of every one as it passed over them. Stunning the excitable into silence.

"May I remind you this is a court of law, not a country fair. The cold eyes of Judge Blackford swept over the public gallery. At all times you will conduct yourself with the decorum the occasion demands or as God is my witness. I'll have the first person to try my patience out of that gallery and into a prison cell for 30 days before they know what's hit them." The cold eyes held the gallery for a few moments more before glancing down to the well of the court where his clerk stood ready.

"Let us begin Mr Quiller."

"Bring the prisoner up."

Despite the Judges stern warning the tension in the court rose perceptibly as footsteps sounded on the stone steps leading up from the holding cells beneath the courtroom. The rattle of chain on stone changing to a dry clunk as those same chains dragged across the two wooden steps up to the dock. A semi-circular wood panelled construction, similar in appearance to a church pulpit. Standing two steps lower than the judges lofty perch, the dock stood directly opposite the judge's bench. Separated by a distance of no more than 20'. The well of the court the preserve of the clerk and counsel for the prosecution. Their assistants ranged about them behind small wooden desks. The principal witness seated to one side beneath the overhang of the balcony like public gallery. They were few in number. Constable Hollins, Sergeant Crane, the midwife, Mrs Potts, and the bearded fisherman Isaac Punce. All sitting quietly awaiting their entry onto the courtroom stage, where the fate of Maudy Jiller would be decided by the evidence they gave to supplement Constable Hollins's case report. The jury ranged along the opposite wall in two banks of six. Sober steady men of affairs. Selected from the local business community.

Two things struck Constable Hollins as Maudy Jiller's head and shoulders appeared into view. Her lower body hidden behind the dock. The first was the light in her eyes. They were brown he knew but the glow from within the sunken sockets seemed almost black against the waxy paleness of her skin. The second was her build. Stripped of her bonnet, shawls and layers of skirts, the simple grey coloured, one piece smock dress she wore only served to highlight her cadaver like appearance. Every inch of skin stretched taut over prominent bones. Her head and face a death mask. Blue lipped and fleshless. Strands of greasy hair tied back with a simple white ribbon. Her neck rising from the straight neckline of the shift corded and taut like the heavy ropes stored in Bonecreake's rope shed. Every vein and muscle displayed. Hands and forearms. Long fingered sticks of bone encased in overstretched pale skin. The grey smock dress hanging to her elbows like a shapeless sack, giving the impression of a loose sail awaiting a breeze to blow it over and away. The heavy handcuffs and connecting chain out of proportion to the thin wrists they restrained. Hidden shackles round her ankles equally as disproportionate to their wearers build. Fear of the prisoner's violent disposition evidenced by the presence of two burly prison officers, stationed at the foot of the wooden steps behind her. Ready, if required, to restrain their charge should anything untoward occur.

For a brief second all was still as every eye except her own turned their gaze on Maudy Jiller. Her appearance sending chills through those who saw only the chains and grey dress. Mrs Potts dabbed her eyes with a scrap of handkerchief, saddened to see a friend so reduced. Isac Punce shivered in his seat and Sergeant Crane eased his still bandaged arm, the knife held in those manacled hands slicing down to bone too recent to be forgotten. Only Constable Hollins remained impassive. To him Maudy Jiller's physical appearance was no more than a distraction to what lay beneath. Her crimes were common knowledge and the likely hood of her sentence a foregone conclusion in the eyes of the masses. What troubled Constable Hollins was a nagging sense of unease that he had missed something. Now in court hearing, the charges read out, Constable Hollins felt the confusion in his thoughts relent as realisation hit him that he had indeed missed something. Several Somethings in fact. So wrapped up in the investigation to recover the children's missing bodies was he that he had allowed another serious crime to slip through the net. The sound of raised voices across the court rousing him from his thoughts as Mr Quiller acting as clerk of the court read out each of the charges laid against the defendant. The formal language of the accusations lending weight to their seriousness. The newspaper reporters scribbling furiously in their note pads as Mr Quiller ending his summary began again by asking the defendant how she pled to each individual charge.

"To the charge of interfering with a corpse, how do you plead. Guilty or not guilty?"

The court waited expectantly for Maudy Jiller to confess her guilt.

In the dock Maudy Jiller stared across the space between herself and Judge Blackford. The dry rattle so familiar to Constable Hollins grating on the ears.

"Don't make no difference what I say. You all want me hung so there's no point me pleading anything. You fine gentlemen can suit yourself as far as I'm concerned."

Gasps of surprise echoed from the gallery and Judge Blackfords colour rose alarmingly beneath his powdered wig.

"Mrs Jiller. It is your right to enter no plea at all. In which case I shall assume you plead not guilty. But it is not your right to question the impartiality of this court. You will be given a fair hearing and equal opportunity to defend yourself. Now I ask you again how do you plead. Guilty or not guilty?"

"If it suits you, sir, not guilty."

"To the charge of cannibalism. How do you plead? Guilty or not guilty?"

"Not guilty. I never ate a shred of meat from those bodies."

"To the charge of attempted murder in that you did assault a police officer with a bladed weapon. How do you plead? Guilty or not guilty?"

"Not guilty. He had hands on my children."

For nearly 20 minutes Mr Quiller was on his feet. Maudy Jiller pleading not guilty to every charge laid before her. The crowded gallery agog at the prospect of the monster of the marshes defying the reality of her situation.

"Mr Jebon."

A bewigged barrister with prominent red veined nose, rose to his feet as Judge Blackford spoke.

"Are you ready to present the case for the prosecution?"

"I am, your honour."

"Then, please, proceed."

"Thank you, your honour."

Now as thin as Maudy Jiller was, Mr Jebon was not. Beneath his wig, flesh rolled down from his forehead to his ankles. Everything about the man shouted excess. His face had a melting quality as if his features were sliding down over his chin. Piggy eyes, broad nose, red petulant lips. All merging to flow into an indistinguishable neck. Spreading sideways over his shoulders to continue its downward flow into and across a massive overhanging stomach and equally precipitous buttocks. His massive thighs overhung with roll upon roll of his own body. His lower legs as round as small wine barrels. Perched atop feet as flat as the floorboards, he stood on. As Maudy Jiller rattled, Mr Jebon whistled. His speech between gasps of air, high-pitched, vaguely girlish. Breathing in, his breath gurgled in his over worked lungs. Breathing out through his flat nose. He whistled like a soon to boil kettle. An altogether bizarre sound to compliment his corpulent appearance. There would be no courtroom theatrics from Mr Jebon. Where he stood was where he stayed. A sweating monument to thirty years of rich living. Hardly able to walk unaided.

One pudgy fist resting on his assistant's small desk Mr Jebon gave a brief outline of the prosecution's case against the defendant Maudy Jiller. Taking his time between gasps to paint a picture in the jury's collective mind of a phantom like figure stalking the hamlet of Bonecreake. Rising up out of the snow laden mist to prey on the misery of others to slake her hunger for human flesh. Violent and murderous in her attempt to evade capture. A monster likely to have continued in her blasphemous feasting but for the sterling work of the police in apprehending her. At no little risk to their own safety.

"I ask you, gentlemen, of the jury."

An arm, the size of a bacon ham, raised and a sausage like finger pointed across the space between his position and the dock.

"Have you ever seen a more evil creature in all your life? Her very appearance is offensive to any right-thinking man."

Here the arm lowered and Mr Jebon was forced to pause for a second, his breath coming in rapid gulps.

"Do not be deceived by what you see, gentlemen." Mr Jebon was back on the attack again. "What you see is an illusion as surely as if this monster was appearing in a child's magic show. I ask you. Please, do not be deceived by her disguise of starvation. She has blood on her hands, gentlemen. Blood on her hands, in her mouth and down deep inside her where innocent youth fed her vile appetite for human flesh."

Again Mr Jebon was forced to pause. The face atop the mountain of rolling skin aglow. Purplish red and bathed in perspiration. Legs all a tremble as he exerted himself to excite the jury to his cause. Every neck in the public gallery craned forward.

"You think me melodramatic, gentlemen, you think me too strident in my opinion? Well, you shall have every opportunity to hear from the mouths of those responsible for her detection and arrest. From those she deceived and those she attacked and left in fear of their lives. Disfigured to this day by her reckless disregard for law and order."

For a moment only the gurgle and whistle of the Mr Jebon's laboured breathing was heard. The rest of the room silent. Hanging on every word.

"With your permission, your honour. The sweating features turned slightly to look up in the direction of Judge Blackford. I would like to call Constable Hollins to the stand."

"Proceed, Mr Jebon."

At the sound of his name Constable Hollins squeezed his hands into tight fists and released the tension he felt as he stood and walked the four steps up to and into the witness box, situated to Judge Blackfords right hand. Standing hands behind his back. Constable Hollins found himself at an angle. In plain view of both the dock and the judges' bench. Mr Jebon taking the time to turn about from addressing the jury face on to positioning himself between the witness and the defendant, supporting himself with his meaty fist as he adjusted his position while Constable Hollins undertook, bible in hand. To tell the whole truth and nothing but the truth so help me God.

"Constable Hollins, I have read the report detailing your investigation into the missing children of Bonecreake and the subsequent arrest of the defendant. For the benefit of the gentlemen of the jury, would you please give the court a summary of your investigation?"

Feeling every eye on him Constable Hollins breathed deeply and fixed his eyes on the watch chain hanging across one of the juror's waistcoat. For the next 15 minutes his eyes never left that point as he spoke clearly and concisely. Never deviating from the facts. The whole court taking in every word. The public gallery silent as the grim details of the search, and subsequent discovery of the missing children's remains unfolded. The arrest of Maudy Jiller. The injuries sustained by her captors and the death of her own daughter occasioned gasps of horror from the gallery that died on the lips under Judge Blackford's scowling stare.

"Thank you, Constable."

Mr Jebon stood solemnly for a few moments, considering his words carefully.

"Constable Hollins. When you arrived in Bonecreake to begin your investigation did you find the inhabitants welcoming?"

Constable Hollins paused for a second before answering.

"Welcoming, yes, but more relieved than anything."

"How so inquired, Mr Jebon?"

"The people of Bonecreake live simply and ply their trade without undue drama. The circumstances, they found themselves in, were beyond anything they had ever encountered before. My presence in uniform steadied them and my direction gave purpose to their willingness to assist me any way possible."

"And yet, Constable, your report states that in the early stages of your investigation one person was reluctant to assist you. In fact you had to take a firm hand and insist. Is that not so?"

"Yes. That is so."

"Constable Hollins, please, tell the court who that reluctant person was."

"The defendant. Maudy Jiller."

The name dropped into the silence of the court like a stone dropped into a duck pond. Every head in court turning to stare at the dock where the manacled defendant stared straight back at them. Seemingly unfazed by the ripples of distaste hanging in the air around her.

"I see," whistled Mr Jebon. Yet only a short while later walking to Old Tom's cottage, this reluctance slipped away and the defendant was most talkative. Describing old Tom and his habits, her general distrust of his character, labelling him a drunkard and so forth.

"Yes, that is the case," agreed Constable Hollins. "In general conversation as we walked with Mr Punce, to and from the old Tom's cottage. She needed little encouragement to join in and speak freely."

"Strange, wouldn't you say, Constable, that a woman who only minutes before had refused to accompany you was now using the opportunity to cast aspersions on the character of one of her neighbours. Damning an innocent man as a lecherous, untrustworthy drunkard whose death was no cause for sadness or pitiful compassion. Ridiculing Mr Punce as a fool for believing otherwise."

"I was surprised by her animosity towards old Tom," agreed Constable Hollins staring down at the sweating face of Mr Jebon. "Noting the broken veins speckling the barrister's nose. I put it down to a clash of personalities. There being no reason at the time to do otherwise."

"Indeed." Constable. Mr Jebon swivelled on his heel and pointed a sausage like finger across the court to the dock. At the time there was no reason to do otherwise and yet in hindsight I believe this conversation shows us all. Here, Mr Jebon directed a meaningful look at judge and jury. That the defendant is a duplicitous, mean hearted creature. A vicious gossip. Willing to use any means at her disposal to cast suspicion on others. Portraying herself as a decent hardworking widow solicitous of her children's welfare. When all the while the wickedness of her actions caused misery and grief to families already mourning the loss of their loved ones."

For all that these were the opening salvoes in the crowns case against Maudy Jiller they had hit the target square on at their first attempt. To a man the jury sat stone-faced. Maudy Jillers bad character firmly established in their collective minds. The rest of the court equally sombre. The only noise the gentle clink of a water carafe against the glass held in Mr Jebon's meaty grasp. His vocal exertions sending runnels of sweat down his lard like chin.

The rest of the morning came and went in a similar vein. Mr Jebon's hammering away at the central theme of vilifying the defendant at every opportunity. Constable Hollins stood down after his stint in the witness box took proceedings up to a break for lunch. Every page of his report providing ammunition for Mr Jebon's judicial artillery, Mrs Potts, the midwife, shy and flustered at being the centre of so much attention. Tearfully explaining her role in sorting the mutilated bodies and her suspicions at the appearance of the bones and lack of flesh, Judge Blackford pausing proceedings to give her time to compose herself while Mr Jebon drained several glasses of cool water and mopped his sweating brow with a linen handkerchief the size of a small tablecloth. The public gallery hanging on every word as the newspaper reporters scribbled furiously in their notebooks. The defendant standing throughout. Silent, unemotional. Hands resting on the parapet of the dock to support the weight of the heavy handcuffs round her wrists. A sketch artist at the back of the public gallery balancing his pencils on his knees while he captured the scene on paper. Maudy Jiller. A wraith like figure in lead and charcoal.

"Sergeant Crane. In your own words would you please describe your actions when you arrived at the defendant's cottage on the morning of the funeral service?"

Like Constable Hollins before him Sergeant Crane gave his reply in a steady clear voice. Sticking to the facts as he outlined his arrival accompanied by Isac Punce. The fisherman, acting as Constable Hollins's messenger, explaining the constable's plan as he rowed the sergeant and himself down the river from nearby Braston to arrive in Bonecreake at first light where they concealed themselves close by until they observed the defendant leave her home to attend the funeral of those lost in the winters cold. After a suitable wait to make sure they were unobserved and the defendant was well away from the scene. They had presented themselves at the cottage door whereby Sergeant Crane in his official capacity had demanded entrance. At first the two daughters had kept silent hoping to remain undiscovered but upon hearing Isac Punce's familiar voice assuring them all was well. They had at last opened the barred door and allowed the men entrance.

"I see." Mr Jebons leaned heavily on his assistant's desk. The effort of standing as the day drew on creasing the lard like forehead with lines of discomfort. "The daughters were left alone in the property?"

Sergeant Crane agreed they were and went on to explain how with himself, acting as witness. Isac Punce had engaged both girls in conversation, explaining that they were required to join their mother at the funeral service, implying without actually saying so that their mother had asked Isac Punce to escort them. Knowing Mr Punce as they did, the girls accepted this and busied themselves dressing in their warmest boots and shawls.

"As to the cottage, what did you find there?" questioned Mr Jebon.

"Nothing out of the ordinary," replied Sergeant Crane. "Although I did think the family where well blessed with cooking pots and oil lamps."

"Items which were later identified as the property of the deceased known as old Tom," stated Mr Jebon's with another meaningful glance at the jury.

"Quite so, sir."

"Carry on, please, sergeant."

"While we walked to the cemetery Mr Punce engaged the girls in general conversation, explaining to them that as I was a stranger in these parts, I had no idea how hard or how long it snowed and what the cold was like. It took but little encouragement for them to both chatter away without care. Mr Punce guiding the conversation to how hungry he was with little to eat and an empty belly. Here the girls grew more guarded in their answers till Mr Punce suggested to them that the stews and soups he made with what little he had were likely the best to be had in Bonecreake. Probably better than anything the girls had enjoyed."

"And they took the bait?" inquired Mr Jebon?

"Yes, sir, they did. From their own lips in all innocence they praised their mothers cooking to high heavens. Such was the magnificence of their winter stews and broths. Tender meats and plenty of wood for the fire to warm their cottage. Sometimes at night when their mother thought them asleep, she would go out into the snow and darkness and return later with more meat which she stored under the snow to freeze and keep fresh. Fetching in a little at a time to cook over the fire."

"I see." Mr Jebon's shifted from one foot to the other to relieve his aching legs. "In your opinion, Sergeant, would it be fair to say that neither daughter had any idea they were eating human flesh?"

"No, sir, they had no idea what they were eating except that it tasted good and there was plenty of it."

An audible shudder went around the court as the full horror of the Sergeant's matter of fact answer curdled the emotions of the packed courtroom. The scribbling pencils pausing as the crowd drew its collective breath.

"Thank you, Sergeant Crane, and now if you please, I would like to turn to matters arising from the unseemly melee within the cemetery. You were badly injured where you not?"

"I was injured, sir, though not so badly that I will not mend."

"Given the circumstances, Sergeant, that is most fortunate. From Constable Hollins's description of events you could just as easily have been killed as injured. Again the meaningful glance at judge and jury as the barrister whistled the point home over pursed lips. Little thought your assailant gave to your safety when she set about you, knife in hand."

Again cannon balls fashioned from Maudy Jiller's past violent actions rained down around her. Mr Jebon acting as breech and barrel to deliver salvo after salvo. The jury keeping mental score of every direct hit.

The final witness of the day filled the witness box with his bulk. Barely disguised by his flowing salt and pepper beard Isac Punce's injured nose and mouth had healed somewhat since his encounter with Maudy Jiller's forehead. However, three front teeth had been lost and one side of his nose showed a ragged assortment of bite marks and indentations where Mrs Potts had set to with her sewing needle. Bringing the gaping flap of skin near torn off by the grinding teeth of his assailant, back roughly in line with the other side of his nose. Both lips still healing beneath scabs of purple and blue mottling.

"Mr Punce, it is plain to see that you have suffered grievously at the hands of the defendant that a man of your size and strength could be so abused by a woman purporting to be half starved is almost beyond belief."

Every head in the public gallery nodded in agreement.

Mr Jebon paused for a couple of whistling breaths. The court all agog at Isac Punce's battered visage.

"However, it is your conversation with the defendant's two daughters that interests me at present."

Isac Punce stood patiently. Aware every eye was on him as the sketch artist leaned back in his seat to get a better view of the fisherman's injured face.

"In the course of your conversation with the two girls, did you feel they were at all times truthful in their speech?"

"They were truthful. The answer as simple as it sounded."

"You are absolutely sure of that, Mister Punce?"

"I am," responded the fisherman. "There was no point in them lying. They were innocent of any wrongdoing and had nothing to gain from spinning me a tale. Besides, I would have spotted a lie in moments and well those girls knew it. They were truthful and answered my questions honestly I am sure of it."

"Thank you, Mr Punce." The melting face of Mr Jebon looked across to the jury. His pressing of Isac Punce on the question of the girl's honesty leaving the 12-assembled men in no doubt as to their mother's guilt. "You may step down."

Later that evening in the light of a low turned oil lamp Constable Hollins sat in his shirtsleeves and stockinged feet. The events of the day food for his inquisitive mind as he filtered his time in court, through a fine sieve of self-analysis. Watching the overweight Mr Jebon at work. It was obvious to the seated constable that the biggest part of the prosecutor's work had been done for him. The facts of the case and supporting evidence afforded no hope of a not guilty verdict. The sustained and seemingly successful attack on Maudy Jiller's character had left everyone in court in no doubt she was a violent, scheming, monster. The crowds who'd arrived seeking entertainment as someone less fortunate than themselves had their dirty linen washed in public. Had all left in sombre mood. The enormity of the crimes and the harsh reality of actual physical evidence captured in the battered face of Isac Punce, had deflated the amusement and left a realism in its place that dried any laughter on the lips.

"We do our work in the gutter of honesty." Sergeant Crane's words very apt after seeing the court in action. For his own part, Constable Hollins had another matter relating to the case to deal with. How to proceed had troubled him for a while. Yet now in the restful atmosphere of his rooms he had come to a decision. When the trial was over he would seek an audience with Maudy Jiller. There were questions yet remaining unanswered about events in Bonecreake. He wished to clear up.

****

The scene outside the court the following morning was one of organised impatience. Captain Blades had his men organised at first light. Formed into two cordons around the front of the building, everyone had to pass through the outer cordon to gain entry into the second before being allowed into the court building. There would be no repeat of the near riot of yesterday. Once every seat in the public gallery had been accounted for and the gentlemen of the press accommodated that was that. No one, whatever their social status was allowed access, they could complain all they liked and many did but Captain Blades was immovable.

Within the court the same scenario was re-enacted as the morning before. His Honour Judge Blackford made his painful way from his chambers up to his raised seat. Joints afire with every step. Scowling the court into silence as those fortunate to pass through Captain Blades's cordons settled down. The sketch artist and the press poised. Pencils at the ready. Mr Jebon. Whistling softly like a simmering kettle on the hob. Seated on sturdy stool like a barrel of congealed cooking fat in his black gown. Sweating under his powdered wig. The twelve men of the jury stern faced. The witnesses solemn faced under the gallery. All sat in silence as the Judge Blackford settled himself.

"Proceed, Mr Quiller."

"Bring the prisoner up."

As before, the heavy chain connecting the ankle shackles grated across the stone steps as Maudy Jiller made her way up from small holding area between the basement cells and the court. Changing to a dull thud as she mounted the two wooden steps leading into the dock. Flanked again by two burly guards she appeared as before. A chained skeleton of a woman.

Shapeless in the ill-fitting grey smock dress. Hair tied back from her gaunt face with same white ribbon. The heavy iron of the restraints around her stick like wrists, resting on top off the wooden rail running round the top of the dock. Her appearance sending a chill through those coming face to face with the Beast of Bonecreake for the first time.

Yesterday Mr Jebon had held the floor unchallenged. Today was Maudy Jiller's chance to speak her piece. The crowd where all ears as Judge Blackford began to speak.

"Prisoner at the bar. At the beginning of these proceeding you entered a plea of not guilty to all the charges laid against you. Having heard the details of the prosecution's case against you, supported by witness testimony and the detailed report of the police investigation into the matter. I feel I must ask. In the face of what seems to be overwhelming evidence against you, do you stand by your original plea of not guilty as charged on all counts? If your plea is unchanged then now is the time to present your defence for consideration by the jury. If, however, you wish to change your plea to one of guilty as charged on all counts then now is the time to do so."

It was at this time the phrase that was to become a byword for the tension of the moment was hurriedly scribbled down by one of the assembled reporters.

Satan himself paused to hear the beast's response.

"Before I answer, may I ask a question, sir?"

The pent-up breath of the public gallery came out in an audible whoosh of air as Maudy Jiller took everyone by surprise.

Judge Blackford let it go as he gave the cadaverous figure in the dock his full attention.

"Yes, you may as long as your question is relevant."

"Thank you, sir. I believe it is." The rattle in Maudy Jillers chest had worsened since her stay in the confined atmosphere beneath the court.

"My question is a simple one, sir."

Again the court held it collective breath.

"Will I be able to talk to the court open and honest if I change my plea to guilty or will you just send me back to the cells and dispose of me as you see fit?"

If Judge Blackford was surprised at the question he didn't show it. He answered without hesitation,

"If you decide to change your plea to guilty, you will forfeit all right to mounting a defence of any kind. However, if you do so, I will allow you leave to speak in open court, providing you use the opportunity wisely and keep your remarks relevant to the matter at hand. Should you indulge in any form of acrimonious rambling's, I will immediately put a stop to your address. Is that clear?"

"Yes sir, thank you sir."

"Now I ask you again. To all the charges laid against you, do you wish to change your plea?"

Under the overhang of the public gallery, Mrs Potts gripped hold of Isac Punce's forearm to steady herself as she perched on the edge of her hard chair. Her handkerchief squeezed into a tight ball in her other hand as she looked across the court to the dock where her friend and neighbour weighed her choice carefully. Admit guilt and face the worst the court could throw at her. Or fight it out and try in some way to prove her innocence against impossible odds. A choice stark enough to shake any hardened villain, let alone a rural fishwife turned reluctant penny dreadful celebrity. Beast of Bonecreake indeed.

When it came the answer had pencils flying across notepads in an instant.

"I am guilty, sir. Guilty of all it."

For a few seconds the court was all noise and no matter Judge Blackfords scowl and cries of order. The public gallery was all astir. In the well of the court Mr Jebon whistled out noisily, what passed for a smug smile breaking out amongst the damp folds of his slab like face. His assistant plying the water carafe with a shaking hand. Mrs Potts gasp of oh Maudy carried across the court but went unheard in the general stir. Her grip on Isac Punce enough to bunch the material of his jacket into folds beneath her fingers. Sergeant Crane and Constable Hollins exchanged glances as the sergeant nodded to his junior. "Well done, Hollins."

In the dock Maudy Jiller closed her eyes and breathed slowly and deeply. Forcing air into her rattling chest. The iron about her ankles and wrists cold and heavy. Chafing against bone, there being little flesh to afford any padding. Around her, the noisy courtroom began to settle, but Maudy Jiller remained silent until judge Blackford having restored order invited her to proceed.

The brown eyes that once stared out across the expanse of the estuary where endless skies met the marshes over the junction of the River Welland and the North Sea. Now turned their unblinking gaze on the twelve men of the Jury. During Constable Hollins's testimony, Maudy Jiller had watched closely. Noting the unwavering gaze of the constable on what seemed to be one member of the jury. Quick to learn she'd decided to adopt the same technique, but with one subtle variation. Standing in the dock Maudy Jiller raised her head. Turned slightly and stared straight at the faces in the public gallery. Her stare unsettling many under her scrutiny, she finally settled on a woman in a dark blue dress and matching bonnet, who returned her stare without flinching. No more than thirty years old, she held the arm of a similar aged man Maudy Jiller took to be her husband. It was to this couple, the woman in particular to whom Maudy Jiller addressed her opening remarks.

"I am Maudy Jiller," the rattling voice echoed around the court. A widowed mother of three children. "Before I did what I did. I lived all my life in Bonecreake and worked for an honest wage in the fishing business of that place."

Constable Hollins's eyebrows rose in surprise at this opening statement. Three children? No one had ever mentioned another child.

"Did you ever ask, Hollins?"

"No, sir."

"Then there is your answer."

"As you can see. I am but a poor figure of a woman, but I was not always so. Once I was young and well-made, carefree as any other youngster growing under their parents' care. I was as any of you. Innocent of hardship and evil. Open hearted and happy to be so."

Maudy Jiller's stare never left the woman in the blue dress.

"Then a terrible misfortune overcame my happiness when my mother died in childbirth. Taken by some complication that saw her die in my father's arms. The baby that would have been my sister dead in her belly. I knew sadness then. Sadness I never knew existed. Sadness that took my father away from me as he cried in the nights. Shouting my mother's name in the darkness. So wrapped up in his grief he forgot about me for days at a time."

A single tear rolled down Mrs Potts face as old unwelcome memories stirred within her. Isac Punce grim faced beside her.

"Of course life goes on and I kept growing. My father never re-married, though he had the chance a time or two. Your mother was all to me Maudy. That's what he used to say. She was all and I want no other. He never did well after we lost her. He worked of course. He had to as bills don't pay themselves and moneys always needed. He fished and took shellfish when he could get them while I tended the home and learned the skills of a fishwife from the woman working ashore."

The reporter's pencils flew across their notebooks and the sketch artist took pains to capture the light and shade around the speaking figure. Except for the dozing figure of Mr Jebon, dreaming of his lunch. The whole court hung on her every word.

"I was near my eighteenth year when my father drowned. An accident people say but I've never been sure. I reckon to this day his heart was so broken he just couldn't carry on. I reckon he'd only been waiting for me to grow big enough to fend for myself before he ended his misery. His body was washed up on the marshes a couple of days after he went missing. His boat found drifting in the wash with no one aboard."

Another tear followed the first down Mrs Potts face. The material of Isac Punces jacket under severe strain as memories of the day Maudy Jiller's father had gone missing resurfaced.

All of Bonecreake had turned out to search both land and sea in the vain hope he might be found alive. All to no avail.

"I lived alone then. For many years, I kept my own company. Too frightened to share my life with anyone, in case they were taken away before their time. I'd had my share of heart break and sadness and wanted no more of it. I worked and I slept and kept myself to myself until I foolishly let loneliness betray me into fancying, I had fallen in love with a man who sweet talked his way into my heart and into my bed with honeyed words and stolen kisses."

The hazel eyes staring back at Maudy Jiller from beneath the dark blue bonnet in the public gallery blinked. Just once but it was enough to signify to Maudy Jiller she was beginning to break through. This woman was on the verge of empathy, although by the way she sat close and laid her arm over her husbands, it appeared her union was a happy one. Maudy Jiller's was not.

"Though he was pleasant and kind in his ways he became too fond of the bottle. Said he needed a drink to steady him now and then. I suppose it was there to be seen but my head was turned and before I knew it his boots were beneath my bed and his ring shiny on my finger."

"This is all very interesting but I fail to see any relevance to your current situation." Judge Blackford interrupted. "If there is any point to this summary of your life history. I strongly advise you to make it."

"Thank you, sir." Maudy Jiller bobbed a small curtsy. The manacles at her wrists loud as they rattled against the woodwork of the dock.

"Well, to cut a long story short my new husbands liking for the bottle became more and more his reason for rising each day until it became all he cared about. He worked and worked hard but it all went on drink. Me and the children saw little of it. Our reward for his labours was the back of his hand and harsh words should I dare to complain. We'd been wed eight years and I had my girls and a boy also in that time, so I had three mouths to feed aside of my own. My husband preferring drink over food to the point where we had nothing. Maudy Jiller stared at the dark blue dress in the public gallery. Nothing at all."

The woman blinked once more. Her expression softening a little as Maudy Jiller's rattling voice carried round the silent courtroom. Silent except for the low whistle of Mr Jebon's tortured breathing.

"Our son died when he was seven. Three days after the new year had turned. Cold it was, bitter cold and us with no food in the house nor firewood either. All our money spent on drink. My husband trapped in nightmares of his own making without the money to buy more. Trembling and sweating. Lashing out right and left. When our boy needed him most, he was blubbering like a baby and beating me because I wouldn't make a whore of myself for the price of a bottle of spirits. All the while our precious little boy was slipping away. Ravaged by illness and starved of nourishment, he was half the size he should have been and had no strength to bear the fever that burned through his body. Bless him he died hungry and sick in my arms, while his father went from house to house begging a glass to steady his nerves."

This was strong stuff and no mistake. The tears running freely down Mrs Potts face, testimony to the memory of Maudy Jiller's husband on his hands and knees in the snow, crying and whining at her door, while his boy lay dying. As fresh in her mind as her husband's voice ordering the drink sodden wretch, to seek his salvation elsewhere, and bother them no more. Every door closed to his alcoholic pleadings.

Maudy Jillers eyes looked into the heart of the women in the dark blue dress. The matter-of-fact sadness in her words coiling round the woman's emotions. Hazel eyes under her dark blue bonnet blinking in quick succession as her lips parted in a silent sigh, saddened by the futility of Maudy Jiller's dismal marriage.

Pausing for a moment to gather her thoughts Maudy Jiller let the sadness in her story sink in. Around the court there were several who were visibly disturbed at her tale, whilst others nodded their heads sagely. The dangers of strong drink taken in excess, demonstrated once again at great cost to those directly affected. An all too familiar tale.

"People in Bonecreake thought it a sadness when our son died but there were few who mourned when my husband passed away a year later. To be truthful I shed no tears."

The sudden note of defiance in Maudy Jillers voice made the rattle more pronounced.

"If those shocks anyone here present, then I have no apologies to offer. Beaten, starved, penniless and desperate. I had had enough. I married because I thought myself loved. Now cruelly used I had long since realised that foolish womanly notion of love had betrayed me. Worse still, it had betrayed my children to the death of one and the likely ruination of the others. No more, I said to myself. No more."

The sketch artist and the reporters hung on every word. Even Judge Blackfford's preoccupation with his painful joints, eased into the background as he listened intently. A feeling there was more to this story than met the eye, growing on him. He was not too be disappointed.

"Once I had made up my mind it seemed only moments before an opportunity to put an end to our suffering presented its self. Sodden with spirits my husband fell into a stupor on our bed. I prodded him and tried to rouse him but he was so far gone to be senseless to all my efforts to wake him. To this day I still wonder why I waited so long but I suppose he had to drive every ounce of love out of me before my heart was sufficiently hardened against him to do what I did."

"And what did you do?" asked Judge Blackford.

Without turning her face away from the blue-dressed woman, Maudy Jiller answered calmly,

"I put a pillow over my husband's face and pressed my weight down upon it until he stopped breathing. I killed him, sir. I murdered my husband."

Mrs Potts cried aloud and slipped sideways off her chair to fall faint over Constable Hollins's knees. The hem of her skirts wafting over the highly polished police issue boots as she fell. Almost completely but not quite as her grip on the sleeve of Isac Punce's jacket saved her. Leaving one arm suspended in mid-air as the back of her bonnet rubbed down the side of the Constables clean shaven, face to hang loosely against his ribcage. Isac Punce an immovable anchor for the stricken midwife, open-mouthed in surprise.

It was the same all around the court as the frank admission of murder caught everyone off guard. Several members of the press had near torn their notepads in half and the sketch artist had considerable difficulty retrieving his pencils and charcoal sticks from the floor of the public gallery. Some people on their feet, others stunned into horrified silence.

Mr Jebons woke from his doze to the sound of breaking glass. His assistant elbowing the water carafe to the floor as he jumped in surprise. Water running freely along the seams of the floorboards beneath his feet.

In the dock the space was limited but both the burly wardens charged with keeping their prisoner in order where on their feet and by Maudy Jiller's side in an instant. Grasping her firmly about the elbows as they squeezed into the available space. The skeletal figure of Maudy Jiller almost absorbed into their considerable presence.

Well into the future when he had retired to write his memoirs. Judge Blackford would remember Maudy Jiller's admission of murder as clearly as the sound of the shattering crystal of Mr Jebon's water carafe. A brief moment in time when his arthritis was completely forgotten and the uproarious scenes going on around him seemed perfectly normal. The feeling lasted only seconds before he called the crowd to order but it stayed with him for the rest of his life.

For now, surprised as the rest of the court, he nonetheless composed himself to address the pale figure standing before him in the dock. The two wardens having pinioned their charge while the court settled its self, now stepped back to their station at the rear of the dock. There being little fear the heavily ironed woman would attempt to escape now order was restored and the court settled back into attentive silence. Maudy Jiller none the worse for their firm handling, standing as before. Manacled wrists resting on the bar of the dock. Facing Judge Blackford now, having broken eye contact with the woman wearing the dark blue dress in the public gallery. The same woman now gripping her husband's arm as tightly as Mrs Potts held fast to Isaac Punce. Both women dabbing their eyes with scraps of handkerchief. Mrs Potts restored to consciousness by a whiff of her own smelling salts passed under her nose a time or two.

"Prisoner at the bar, you have just admitted to deliberately murdering your husband by suffocating him while he slept. I ask you now. Is this confession truthful and not some fantasy you wish you had enacted?"

Without hesitation Maudy Jiller nodded in the affirmative. "It's the truth, sir. As God is my witness. I killed him before his love of the bottle did for us all."

"I see." Judge Blackford's words in the tense silence of the court carried the full weight of the law within them. "You realise that whilst unrelated to the matter at hand. You will have to answer for your actions at a future date and as you have already confessed your guilt to committing a capital crime, the outcome is likely to be the most severe punishment the court can hand down."

"I thought that would be the case, sir but its only right, you know these things about me and I have more to tell yet about what I done and the why of it."

Judge Blackfords eyebrows raised under his wig.

"The more you speak off, is it related to the charges you face concerning the missing children of Bonecreake?"

"Yes, sir. There's a good deal more to talk about that."

Maudy Jiller turned her face away from Judge Blackford and stared across the court to meet Constable Hollins's gaze.

"There's other things to talk about an all as I think constable shiny button's there might already be suspecting me off. Here the court gasped as Maudy Jiller smiled and laughed aloud. A rattling roll of noise like dried peas being shaken in an empty tin. Unnerving and unpleasant in the same breath.

You don't know all despite your cleverness young man but let me carry on, sir…" Here, Maudy Jiller looked back to Judge Blackford, "and I will tell all and be truthful from first to last."

Juddge Blackford nodded. "As I have allowed you to come this far. I see no reason to stop you now. You may continue."

Maudy Jiller as best she was able given the weight around her wrists bobbed a slight curtsy in Judge Blackfords direction. The rattle of chain against wood jarring on the ear. The white ribbon tying back her hair fluttering slightly with the movement of her head. Akin to a butterfly settling to rest.

"Once my husband was gone, our lives were easier. What I earned I put to good use and we had food and firewood. There was no harshness, nor fighting. My girls laughed like children should. I was strict with them mind. They were raised properly to be hard working and respectful in their ways but they were happy enough though times were still hard. We made do with what we had and when we couldn't, I found a way to bring in a bit more."

"A bit more," inquired Judge Blackford.

"Yes, sir, food, money, sometimes both. There were them in Bonecreake, who'd share a little of what they had to help me." Here Maudy Jiller spoke directly across the court to Mrs Potts and Isac Punce. "Many times an extra bowl of something would come from the midwife's cottage to feed the girls or a small basket of fish would come my way to be smoked for winter storage. It was only in the most desperate of times when people had to look to their own and had nothing to share. That no one could help me. Times like last winter when all about was frozen solid. That's when I turned to old Tom and made myself useful about his cottage."

"Useful," inquired Judge Blackford. "What did you do there in the depths of winter that he could not?"

Here Maudy Jiller seemed to pause for a moment as if steeling herself.

"I am a woman, sir. Some would say a poor excuse for one standing here, chained hand and foot. But a woman nonetheless and a woman can always be useful to a man who keeps no wife and likes to pull a cork. Don't forget, I am well-used to the ways of a drunkard. I refused to whore myself for the price of a drink for my husband. To put food in my daughter's belly and a keep a roof over their heads. I abandoned such scruples and did what I had to do."

"I see." Judge Blackford leaned forward across the bench. "This old Tom character used you as a whore and paid you accordingly."

"Yes, sir." Maudy Jiller shook her head as if in regret. "He was a filthy-minded lecher and it was a horrible business but the little he gave me for dancing made all the difference."

"Dancing?"

A look of surprise briefly replaced the near permanent scowl on Juge Blackfords face.

"Yes, sir. Old Tom paid me to strip naked and dance for his amusement whilst he sat and drank from a bottle of spirits. Him being too old and far gone to enjoy pleasuring himself any other way. I danced and he watched. While he drank himself silly and fell asleep in his armchair, then I would take my few pennies and let myself out, leaving him snoring and grunting like the drink sodden pig he was."

In the public gallery the reporters filled notebook after notebook and the sketch artist's pencils flew across his sketch pad capturing every emotion on display. Around him, the public sat transfixed as debauchery followed murder from Maudy Jiller's lips. The woman in the blue dress fascinated and repelled in equal measure as Maudy Jiller's tale unfolded before her. Mrs Potts' awash with uncomfortable memories of half heard rumours. Constable Hollins grim faced. There would be no need to interview Maudy Jiller after the trial. His questions about old Tom being answered in open court.

"I take it this arrangement between yourself and this old Tom character carried on throughout the winter months," inquired Judge Blackford.

"No, sir. Not through the entire winter. It ended when he offered me less and less to entertain him. I suspected he was running out of money yet he still wanted to indulge himself, so I put an end to it."

"You no longer acted as his whore?"

"No, sir. Like my drunkard of a husband before, I danced for the old fool while he drank himself senseless. Then I stuffed his own neckerchief down his throat and choked him. While I pinched his nose tight shut. He struggled a bit but full of drink and old into the bargain he had little strength to save himself. I left the mean-hearted old bastard sat in a pool of his own water in his armchair. Off course, I pulled his neckerchief out his throat after I got myself dressed, so no one would be any the wiser. Then I took all the money he had about him and left him to it."

"By heavens she's a cool one," whispered Sergeant Crane to no one in particular. Constable Hollins's head nodding automatically in agreement. While the rest of the court gasped and shuffled around in their seats. In their wildest dreams no one present could have dreamt that such revelations would be forthcoming. Certainly not Judge Blackford who for the last twenty years sitting in judgement of humanities evils, had never heard the like. Maudy Jiller was breaking new ground in every sense of the word.

"Mr Quiller."

"Yes, your honour." The clerk was on his feet in an instant.

"As difficult as it is given the sordid nature of this morning's business. I trust you are keeping an accurate record of proceedings thus far?"

"Yes, your honour."

Mr Quiller glanced down at the surface of his assistant's small desk, where a heavy ledger used to record the business of the court lay open. The assistant's spidery hand writing filling the blank pages within.

"Please make a note to leave the day after tomorrow free so that this court might consider the implications of the defendant's multiple confessions." Here Judge Blackford turned to question Maudy Jiller as she stood calmly amidst the buzz of conversation within the court.

"That is of course unless you have any other crimes to confess to which this court will need to consider?"

The ghost of a smile flittered across Maudy Jiller's gaunt features as she answered Judge Blackfords inquiry.

"No, sir. I have no more to answer for other than what I told you about already. I believe that's enough to get me hung twice over."

Judge Blackfords brows knitted together in a frown as he supported his weight on his forearms and shifted his position slightly to ease his aching joints.

"That is yet to be decided but I feel safe in assuring you that the likelihood of a positive outcome is distinctly remote.

However another day's business has no place in today's proceedings. Do you wish to continue addressing the court or has your eulogy run its course."

"Well, there's one or two more things to tell of, sir."

"Very well sighed," Judge Blackford. "Carry on."

Once again Maudy Jiller lifted her head and faced the blue dressed woman in the public gallery. A fact not un-noticed by the sketch artist, who was almost bent double to peer along the row of seats, to sketch a likeness of the woman in question. Her features partially obscured by her bonnet lending an air of mystique to her appearance on the artist's pad.

"It was a while after I killed old Tom that the weather turned from heavy rain to snow. The cold set in so fierce that I had to scour everywhere and anywhere for firewood. Given that old Tom wasn't going to need any warming this side of the grave it made sense to me to strip everything that would burn from his cottage. After all, he used to laugh at me and tell me to dance faster to warm myself when I was naked. Used to call me his dancing bean pole on account of my slim build. So I got my own back. Taking everything he had under the cover of darkness. I was going to sell it all but the snow got so bad I couldn't get out of Bonecreake to find a pawnshop in the town."

"I take it the body of this old Tom was simply left where he died?" asked Judge Blackford.

"Yes, sir, wasn't no point in trying to move him. Stunk to high heavens as it was, all blown up and black round the edges."

Audible gasps from the gallery were stilled in an instant under Judge Blackfords scowl. Only Mr Jebon's whistling breath sounded kettle like across the court. The barrister almost numb from the waist down as his overflowing buttocks weighed heavily on the hard wooded stool.

"At what point did you decide to steal the children's bodies? asked Judge Blackford. "Curiosity growing, despite himself."

"Beginning of February it was, sir. By that time the cupboards were bare and the snow lay deep around. The girls were famished and I was desperate. I'd had one child die in my arms. Starved and ill for want of nourishment. I couldn't bear the thought of my girls going the same way leaving me alone in the world."

A handkerchief dabbed at the hazel eyes under the blue bonnet, as the court hung on every word. Many uneasy at this matter of fact recounting of Maudy Jillers descent into cannibalism.

"I woke one morning to hear the girls crying with cold and hunger. I can hear it now. Cut me to the quick to think I was going to lose them. I cried myself that morning. I was at my wits end when one of them spoke to me about cutting her fingers off and eating one a day before she started on her toes."

This time the gasps and cries from the gallery went unchecked as Judge Blackford let the crowd have its head for a moment, allowing himself time to reflect on the absolute misery Maudy Jiller found herself in.

"It were then that I thought of it, sir. It were then that I decided to do what I did. I knew at least two children had already died. Knowing Bonecreake as I do, it didn't take me long to scout out where they been laid. That night when the girls had cried themselves to sleep, I took one of the fish sledges and loaded the body of a young boy on to it. It was easy enough pulling the sledge along the top of the riverbank. I know every inch of it like the back of my hand and the moon was half-full. So there was enough light to go back and forth. The wind kept the snow thin on top of the bank while it piled it high on the sheltered side. So my footprints and the tracks of the sledge blew away in the blink of an eye. By the time I reached old Tom's, hardly a trace remained of my passing."

"I see." Judge Blackford looked hard at Maudy Jiller. "It did not enter your head that what you were about. Would cause untold misery to the family of the child whose remains you had stolen."

"I thought nothing of it, sir. Sounds bad to say so I know but I had only one thing on my mind. Besides another family's grief, wouldn't ease my own if I stood by and watched my children die."

Judge Blackford made no comment. There was an irrefutable logic to the defendant's answer that defied argument.

"I had to wait a bit for the body to thaw before I could butcher it. Of course it was all new to me, cutting a body up but I've skinned plenty of rabbits and filleted thousands of fish in my time so I soon got the hang of it. Cutting and chopping and what not. Once I got a fire lit and a pot of melted snow on the boil, it became an easy matter to do what was needed and get the various bits in the pot to boil the meat off. As Constable shiny buttons found when they dug out the privy in the yard, I put aside the head, the hands and feet. The girls would have spotted they were eating fingers and toes in an instant, so I couldn't use them. The heads are all bone and the guts were blackened and foul but the limbs and the body served well enough. I broke up some of old Tom's furniture for fire wood and boiled the bones in his cooking pot till the meat fell away. Then I wrapped the meat in sailcloth and buried it in the snow behind my garden wall away from prying eyes. The bones you know I chucked down the privy seemed the best place for them as everywhere else I could have hidden them was frozen solid."

Constable Hollins knew it was all in his mind but for a moment during Maudy Jillers testimony he smelt the earthy smell of the privy in his nostrils and the taste of foulness dry on his lips as the sightless, rat gnawed skull of a child stared up at him from the depths of the bone filled privy.

"The children were happy when they had a hot stew inside them for breakfast, I can tell you. Not much mind because it had to last but they ate it up in an instant and clapped for joy when I told them there was more where that came from. Set them up a treat it did and eased my worries, no end I can tell you. I know what I did was wrong and goes against all that's natural but I'll be damned if I was going to watch my daughters starve like there brother before them. They didn't have to know what they was eating and I took none of it for myself except to drink the hot meat juice from the bottom of the pot to keep me going."

"You repeated this procedure three more times. Is that correct?" asked Judge Blackford?

"Three more times, sir. Yes, that's right enough. I took three more as I needed them and the moon gave me light enough to see by. Chopped them up and boiled them in old Tom's cottage until the firewood ran out. There being no more furniture in his cottage to burn, the last one I had to butcher as best I could. It was still part frozen, so there was a fair bit of meat on the bones when I threw them down the privy. I suppose that's what attracted the rat. The scent of all that meat. He must have had a right feast on all them fingers and toes. The heads and all."

"Yes, thank you. That will be quite enough I think."

Judge Blackford interrupted as the retching sounds of someone unable to contain their horror echoed off the curved woodwork of the court ceiling. A man at the rear of the gallery, excusing himself to stand upright and shuffle through the packed gallery. Pale faced and trembling. The strong smell of his breakfast hanging around him as fresh vomit stained the front of his waistcoat and trousers.

"Seems my stews are not to his liking, sir." The gaunt face looked across from the gallery towards Judge Blackford. "I daresay bacon and eggs is better than boiled bodies but I suppose you have to be starving to appreciate a hot stew of whatever you can get. The sunken eyes cast their baleful glance across the court and settled on the 12 serious faced jurymen. Not that I expect well to do men of affairs like yourselves to have any idea what desperate straits I found myself in. Nor that great whistling lump of lard either."

"That will do," thundered Judge Blackford. "You have had your say."

"I've had my say, sir and I thank you for it but I'd like someone to tell me in all good conscience. How a glutton whose body is so fat and bloated he can hardly stand and 12 well-fed men can sit in judgement on a starving mother. Who did what she did to save her hungry children from a death none of them could hope to understand?"

"Be silent."

Judge Blackford's arthritis flared hot and bright in stabbing needles of pain as his temper rose. His joints afire

105

like old Tom's furniture burning under a cooking pot of bubbling bones. Around the court the mood turned noticeably ugly with accusing eyes staring down at both the prosecutor, struggling to rise from his stool and the members of the jury who exhibited signs of anger and embarrassment at being singled out for criticism.

"We are doing our duty," shouted one frustrated juror. I have known hardship shouted another in his defence."

"Your honour, I must protest." Whistled Mr Jebon loudly as his clerk manfully put his shoulder under one overflowing armpit and hoisted the massive bulk of the prosecutor upright. Mr Jebon scarlet faced with temper and effort. Sweat running freely down his outraged face, giving a waxy sheen to the pasty skin beneath. "This is a disgrace, your honour. I demand you put a stop to this woman's insolence at once."

"Hear hear," shouted another of the jurymen. On his feet as where several of his fellows. "She has no right to insult us because we have done well in life. It's not our doing that she's a murderer."

"And a cannibal," yelled another pointing a clenched fist at Maudy Jiller who stood impassively in the dock. "I say we should string her up now and have done with it."

Beside herself with a sense of injustice that would not be contained. The blue-dressed woman in the public gallery was on her feet taking issue with the enraged jurymen and offended barrister. Her voice laced with tears, yet strong and sharp. Her husband open-mouthed as his wife and several members of the jury, traded insults across the court. Their arguing supplemented by several other women joining in with well-aimed barbs that pricked at the soaking monolith supported by his clerk.

"Look at you, bloated like a beached whale," yelled one.

"She should have boiled your great carcass. You're a disgrace," shouted another.

"One of your breakfasts alone would keep ten families in food for a fortnight."

It seemed every woman present had risen to their feet, intent on venting their anger at the gross figure of the sweating prosecutor. The air full of hostility as women who were normally silent partners to the work of men, unleashed the full fury of their outrage at well fed men judging a starving woman.

"You there yelled one florid-faced juryman at the husband of the blue-dressed woman. What sort of husband are you letting your wife behave like a screaming harpy? Shame on you that you can't keep her in order."

In an instant the husband was on his feet. The very image of offended masculinity.

"Damn you, sir. My wife's opinion of you mirrors my own. You are no more than a group of pompous, self-serving hypocrites. My wife has every right to express herself and does so with my blessing. If I could get among you, I'd give the lot of you the thrashing you so richly deserve for daring to suggest otherwise. Screaming harpy indeed."

"Your honour, I demand."

What Mr Jebon was about to demand no one would ever know as the great colossus shuddered and his breath came in frantic bubbling whistles. Saliva blowing from his gasping mouth as his overloaded respiratory system finally gave up the unequal struggle. The heart encased in layers of fat, beating wildly as the barrister slumped down onto the wooden stool. His clerk bending at the knees as the weight propped up on his shoulders became too much to bear.

"Order," yelled Judge Blackford at the top of his lungs. "Blast and damnation I will have order in court or I'll give every man jack of you a dose of rough justice you won't forget in a hurry. Be seated all of you and keep silent. This is a court of law not an alehouse on a Saturday night."

Amongst the hubbub Maudy Jiller stood quiet and her wardens seeing no need for alarm watched on wonderingly as the drama provoked by their charge unfolded. Likewise. Constable Hollins sat quietly. His eyes firmly set upon the pale figure in the dock. His mind as always assessing the evidence before him. Learning from experience. Although the scenes of disorder in the court where something he never thought to ever experience. Beside him. Sergeant Crane kept calm. Neither officer felt the need to intervene in what was after all, an argument between opposing viewpoints. The protagonists, separated as they were, could trade threats and insults all day long without fear of actually coming to blows. It might be a different matter outside the court when eventually they all exited the building, but other officers were on hand, and Captain Blades would assuredly give short shrift to anyone causing a nuisance without.

No it was the manner in which the disturbance in court, had been formulated, that occupied the Constable's attention. Reminiscent of the fracas at the graveside Maudy Jillers words and actions had caused others around her to become embroiled in a situation not of their making. In the eyes of the law, she was guilty of stealing the dead to feed to the living. Her actions were wrong and she had admitted as much. Leaving aside the double murder confession. There was also the matter of assaulting two police officers in the course of their duty. Obstructing justice. The list seemed endless. That she was guilty seemed to bother Maudy Jiller not at all. That she could provoke a social comparison between her circumstances of abject misery and the obvious prosperity and excess of those given responsibility for meting out the punishment for her crimes. Fascinated the Constable's inquiring mind. A lowly uneducated fishwife Maudy Jiller may be but somewhere inside the skeletal figure lay a natural ability as an orator to provoke emotion. Portraying herself as victim and villain in the same breath. A stroke of genius Constable Hollins was sure would stimulate great debate when the nations newspapers were read at countless breakfast tables, come tomorrow morning. For now though Judge Blackford had had enough. Mr Jebon lay slumped sideways across his stool, propped up against his clerk's small desk, wheezing dangerously, unable to rise. The jurymen and the irate husband were still trading insults and all about the court there was discord and disturbance.

"Mr Quiller"

The clerk rose with what dignity he could muster given the circumstances. Mr Jebon finally managing to draw a short breath without blowing further saliva down his stained front when he exhaled. "Summon the constables without if you please. I'll have the court cleared and the prisoner returned to her cell till we re-convene after luncheon."

The fact that it was barely 11.30 in the morning ignored by the clerk as he ordered the doors opened and the prisoner taken down. Judge Blackford's scowl twisting his features into a knot of anger as blue uniformed constables. Hastily summoned from without. Entered the public gallery and

109

began herding those lucky enough to have seats towards the exit. The enraged women in particular proving difficult to manage.

In the well of the court two blue uniformed figures assisted the stricken barrister to his feet as he struggled for breath and movement in equal measure. Judge Blackford hobbled down from the bench to his private chambers. Hips, knees and ankles aflame with vicious stabs of pain. His sense of outrage sending a flush to his cheeks.

"Well, Hollins." Sergeant Crane stood aside as Mrs Potts and Isac Punce made their way through the door behind their seats that lead into the small room set aside for witness's use. "I never thought to see such scenes in Billy Blackhearts court. I daresay he didn't either answered Constable Hollins. Not your everyday fare, that's for certain."

"No assuredly, not agreed, Sergeant Crane." A rare smile creasing his face. I wouldn't like to be in her shoes when she's bought up for sentencing.

"Quite so." Agreed Constable Hollins. "Quite so."

Sat on the hard wooden bench that served as both seat and bed. Maudy Jiller smiled wistfully. The parchment like skin stretched over her cheekbones relaxing slightly as memories of happier days pushed the raucous morning in court from her mind. Her girls were all to her and now despite losing both. One dead, the other held in an asylum. Shaking silently even now. She could sense them around her like wraiths in the shadowy corners of the grim stone cell. Lights in the darkness that gave a lie to her situation. Fresh as wild flowers picked from the wind-swept river bank. Nature's fresh scent overlaying the foulness of the slop bucket at the back of the cell.

"What's this my darlings," cooed Maudy Jiller rocking at the waist as she sung quietly to herself.

"Flowers, Mummy," whispered soft voices. "Flowers picked just for you."

The tears came then. Running freely from her tired eyes. A rain of sadness that emptied her soul of every emotion. A dam of misery emptying into a river of grief. The sense of loss overwhelming. A mother's natural instinct to care for her young betrayed by accidental death and insanity. To her very core Maudy Jiller knew an all-enveloping sense of despair reserved for mothers unlucky enough to lose the child they nurtured in the womb for nine long months. Doubly so for the rocking figure as both her daughters were ever lost to her.

"There's no coming back from this, Maudy."

"I know, Daddy, but I couldn't let them die. I had to do something."

"I know, my love. More's the pity I couldn't help you but I am here now."

"Daddy, why did you leave me? Was I not worth living for?"

"Maudy sweet Maudy, don't you ever think that, you were my one ray of sunshine in a world of darkened skies. I loved you though my heart was heavy with grief at the loss of your mother. Grief the like of which you're suffering now my little lovely. I was living yet dying a little more every day, for want of your mother's love."

"I'm going to die, Daddy. It's the rope for me and I know it."

"Better that than a life of loss and sadness, Maudy. I'll be waiting when you cross over. Don't you fret. We'll all be together again and happy as before".

Maudy Jiller sniffed as her tears ended and a harsh note crept into her thoughts.

"There'll be no heaven for me, Daddy. The evil I've embraced holds me still. My hearts full of anger and I itch to hold a cushion over the face of that flabby glutton and those bastards sitting over me like the 12 disciples. All holier than thou. I'd slit their throats and butcher all of them for the meat on their well-fed bones. Hypocrite's the lot of them."

"No, Maudy. That's not my sweet little sunshine talking. You don't mean any of that."

A wild smile broke through the gauntness and a loud cackle rattled from the bony chest beneath the grey shift.

"Oh, I mean it, Daddy. I mean it with all my blackened heart. They'd dance under my knife while my girls built the fire high. I'd skin them and gut them and give their livers to the starving. I'd boil the righteousness out of them and let anyone begging their bread, feed on the meat left behind."

Manacled hands squeezed the cold air. Rolling folds of fat in strong bone fingers, reddened and bruised as the prosecutor gasped and whistled. In her agitated imagination. Maudy Jiller squeezed and shouted aloud at the madness of it.

"I'd slice up that great whistling lump of lard and light my way to hell with 10,000 candles made from his blubber. The eyes in the gaunt skull-blazed with anger fuelled by hysteria. Cut strips of the slavering lump and enjoy his screams while he watched bits of himself boil."

"Your honour, I must object."

"Object all you like, you overblown shit house. No one's going to stop me, are they?"

"No," there not shouted the enraged husband jumping to his feet. The women in blue waving and smiling encouragement. "You slice away and be damned to the lot of them. The husband shook his fist as the jurymen danced naked over hot coals. I'll thrash any man that tries to interfere with your pleasure."

"Hear, hear," shouted every other man in the public gallery as their wives and sweethearts waved and shouted encouragement. "Trim a slice for us, Maudy. Make him whistle, Maudy. Slice him up, slice him up," chanted others. Whilst the jurymen danced the faster and their howls and screams grew louder.

"What say you to that, Daddy?" Rattling laughter burst from dry lips and hurried to stoke the fire beneath a giant pot of boiling fat. "What do you say to that?"

The walls kept silent as the rocking woman raved.

"You've gone again then have you?"

Maudy Jiller shouted loudly in anger.

"Well, you might as well. You were never there when I needed you. A father when you wanted to be, then a fool wallowing in his loss. Weak like all the men I've come across."

Maudy Jiller's teeth ground down hard against each other. The skeletal face burning with malice in the sunken eye sockets. Bony fingers gripping tight the unyielding frame of the wooden bench as the barristers sweat soaked skin slipped through her fingers.

"I hope you felt it when you threw yourself into the sea. I hope you felt the cold grab your heart and stab you with the knowledge that the young woman you left behind, wouldn't mourn your loss overlong before she forgot you altogether."

The fall of a heavy footstep and a key turning in the lock of the cell door stilled the rocking figure.

"I'll show those bastards no weakness murmured a hard unfeeling voice somewhere behind the sunken eyes. I'll carry my chains and spit on their graves before they see weakness." Maudy Jiller cried.

The two burly wardens stepped into the small cell.

"It's time," spoke one to the seated figure who looked up at their blank faces beneath the peaked caps.

The manacled figure rose unaided to her feet with a rattle of chain on stone and shuffled between the wardens out of the open cell door. The tear-filled eyes dry. The rocking hysteric steady. Nature hating a vacuum filling the emptiness of her spent grief with a cold purposeful resolve. Maudy Jiller paused in the corridor leading up to the court, breathing deeply before speaking aloud.

"Well, let's be about it then. I wouldn't want to keep his honour waiting."

****

For all that the scenes in court had been noisy and hostile during the morning session. Maudy Jiller climbed up into the dock to an almost funeral silence. Arrayed around the court the Judge and prosecutor with his clerk and other officers of the court were all seated where she expected to see them. Two blue-uniformed witnesses in the shape of Constable Hollins and Sergeant Crane sat in their seats under the overhang of the public gallery. Mrs Potts and Isac Punce's presence no longer deemed necessary. The jury sat stern faced. The public gallery, however. Save for a row of newspaper reporters and the ever-present sketch artist. Was a deserted sea of empty seats. Judge Blackford denying the hostile crowd of the morning, any further opportunity to disrupt proceedings. A strong presence of police constables barring the door to the public, who complained loudly but to no avail.

"Judge's orders. You lot had your fun this morning. Now be off with you and think yourself lucky you didn't end up in the cells keeping the cannibal company."

Now the scene was set for every unsympathetic eye in the court, to be trained on the dock, where the pale figure stared straight back without the slightest show of emotion. The fishwife's eyes as flat and cold as any of the thousands of fish she had filleted in the crude-built fish sheds of Bonecreake. If anyone thought Maudy Jiller broken, they had another thought coming.

Judge Blackford's opening remarks directed at the jury held more than a note of admonishment in them as he spoke. Hard and uncompromising.

"Members of the jury. You have had adequate time to settle yourselves and reflect on your actions during the shameful scenes that marred this morning's proceedings. I am forced to say that none of you behaved in a way that did you credit. Allowing yourselves to be riled by the insults and arguments of the defendant and the public. The Judges scowl grew more pronounced as he warmed to his theme. It will not do gentlemen. It will not do at all. I expect better. Indeed I demand better from men who are supposedly steady minded men of business. When I ask you to retire to consider your verdict, I demand you put all the froth and nonsense of this morning from your minds and address the matter at hand in a dispassionate manner. Weigh the evidence, gentlemen. Weigh the evidence in the scales of sober deliberation and return your verdict accordingly. Nothing else is acceptable. Do I make myself clear?"

To a man the jury sat chastened until the foreman rose to answer.

"Perfectly clear, your honour."

Judge Blackford nodded his head in acknowledgement. Moving slightly in his seat to look straight across the well of the court at the pale figure in the dock.

"The case for the prosecution and statements you made to explain your actions have both been heard in open court. Judge Blackford's scowling face challenging Maudy Jiller to suggest otherwise. It is now my duty to sum up the facts of the matter and give direction where I feel it necessary. So that the members of the jury can reach a verdict on all of the charges laid against you. Be aware that in the event of any unseemly interruption from you. I shall immediately have you returned to your cell and carry on in your absence. Is that clear?"

Maudy Jiller answered without hesitation.

"Yes, sir. Clear as day."

For a few seconds more the judge looked at Maudy Jiller before shifting his weight on his elbows to face the jury.

For the next hour Judge Blackford's deep steady voice filled the court. Punctuated by the odd whistle and wheeze from Mr Jebon. The barrister now sufficiently recovered to sit upright unaided. The members of the jury attentive as they listened. Solemn faced, acting the part of impartial jurors. The fact that at least one had suggested lynching the defendant not three hours previously, conveniently forgotten. From the dock there was nothing but silence. Maudy Jiller stood still as a statue. Seemingly indifferent.

Not so the newspaper reporters scribbling away in their shorthand. The sketch artist concentrating on the Judge as his pencil moved in his hands. Capturing the likeness of the be-wigged figure as he delivered his summing up. Although in truth the summing up was no more than a formality as Maudy Jiller had already changed her plea to guilty. The jury could only return one verdict and it was to this end that the judge directed them.

The jury retiring to consider their verdict seemed almost farcical to Constable Hollins as he watched the 12-men troop out of the court to re-appear barely 30 minutes later. The foreman rising to his feet to pronounce the defendant guilty as charged on all counts.

In the gallery the reporter's filled page after page of shorthand and the sketch artist turned his attention to the defendant. Judge Blackford's likeness captured in pencil and charcoal.

Maudy Jiller, dry-eyed and unemotional, Manacled wrists resting on the wooden rail of the dock.

For all that the judge looked and sounded the part as he handed down the punishment applicable to the crimes. Constable Hollins couldn't help feel the whole episode a complete waste of time. Undermined by Maudy Jiller's confession to murder, the trial had become no more than an exercise in procedure. The sentence's Judge Blackford had just handed down for Maudy Jiller's crimes to date. Would inevitably be over ridden by a death sentence at the hearing scheduled to take place in two days-time. A confession in court to not one but two murders leaving Judge Blackford with no alternative. Maudy Jiller would hang. Probably within the week. All the sympathy for her plight as a woman badly abused and driven by circumstances beyond her control would not save her. The murder of her abusive husband was bad enough in a time when society deemed wives were subservient to their husband's wishes. Murdering old Tom for his few remaining pennies. Unforgivable in the eyes of polite society and the rule of law. Constable Hollnis left the court pleased to be free of the oppressive silence. Maudy Jiller left the court never to be free until the moment of her death. Which the newspapers read around the nation's breakfast tables the following morning, assured their readers would soon be forthcoming. Just how soon they failed to predict. As yet again. Maudy Jiller took the world by surprise and cheated the hangman of his breakfast.

****

For a brief moment Maudy Jiller's hands and feet felt as light as feathers. The warden kneeling by the wooden cot in her cold cell. Gathering up the manacles and adjoining chains from the stone floor. Hardly noticed the angry red welts and open chafed skin around her hunger-shrivelled limbs once the restraints were removed. Prisoners came. Prisoners went. The celebrity status of this particular prisoner meant nothing to the wardens. The situation unusual only in that normally two of their female counterparts would have attended a female prisoner. Maudy Jiller's violent confrontation in Bonecreake cemetery and the nature of the charges laid against her giving those responsible for her incarceration pause for thought. Hence the burly wardens capable of out muscling their charge, should anything untoward excite her volatile nature. Stuff and nonsense as far as both wardens where concerned. Like other prisoners before her. Maudy Jiller. Seemingly cowed by her surroundings in custody was calmness its self. Given to raving in her cell when alone, which was to be expected when the stark reality of her situation was thrust upon her. But other than that no worse than any other unfortunate who had passed through their hands. When that cell door slams shut it bites home. An observation both had heard many times. That's when they realise the right and wrong of it don't matter. You can be as tough as you like. Steel and stone are tougher. Their indifference overwhelming. Under normal circumstances. Maudy Jiller would endure the soul-destroying passage of time as each day rolled into the next. Until death released her from earthly incarceration. As it was with another court appearance in the offing and a double murder confession on the table Maudy Jiller would soon be facing a higher judgement than the Honourable Judge Blackford. An observation one warder made to the other as they settled in the guard room to enjoy their evening meal.

"I reckon this one will be sliding down the sulphur slope as soon as her neck snaps." The other warden didn't pause for thought as he poured strong black tea into two brown mugs.

"She's a bad un sure enough unless he wants to put his boot up her backside, I can't see Saint Peter opening the pearly gates on her account. We see them come. We see them go. Both wardens raised their mugs. Which way they go only the devil and the good lord knows?" The mugs clinked together in a familiar ironic toast.

"You're going to hell, Maudy. The noise began somewhere in the ceiling near the barred slit window as madness induced seagulls squabbled amongst themselves to perch on the window ledge. Taunting the woman below.

There raucous cries given voice. There's a pot boiling to strip the meat from your bones Maudy. The devil's children are grinding their teeth ready to feast on your murderous carcass, Maudy. There waiting and there so hungry, Maudy. They'll eat you, bones and all till there's nothing left. Only they'll take an eternity to bite you and chew you and swallow every rotten mouthful till they shit you out and begin all over again. Can you feel them, Maudy? Wings flapped and webbed feet scrabbled against the stone of the window ledge. Can you feel all those teeth and all that hot burning slaver dripping over you?"

For all that the evil of her desperate actions tormented her. All Maudy Jiller could feel was a great rolling emptiness inside her. A deserted space as bare of emotion as the muddy expanse of the marshes, where the sea met the land at Bonecreake.

"Tide's out, Maudy."

A pale figure struggled upright out of the oozing mud to stand dishevelled in front of her sunken eyes. The drip, drip, drip of mud laden sea water loud against the stone of the cell floor.

"We'll be together again soon, Maudy. The stench of corruption filled the cell as the bloated corpse of her drowned father spoke. I'll save you, Maudy, we'll lie low in the marshes and the devil won't know where to find you my sweetheart. I won't let no one hurt you again."

"If you loved me, woman, you'd go and spread your thighs. I need a drink to steady me a little. Just a glass or two to see me right."

The shade of her husband lurched drunkenly across the cell and pointed an accusing finger from the shadows as old

Tom sat. Bottle of spirits in hand by the imaginary fireplace in the opposite wall to where Maudy Jiller sat. Rocking slowly on the hard wooden bench.

"Dance for me, Beanpole. Let me see them skinny bones a jiggling."

A coarse laugh mingled with her husband's whining voice.

"Spread your thighs woman. I need a drink. Any man will do. Blast you for a heartless crone. Bring me the price of a bottle or I'll thrash the girls and make them scream."

"Dance, your bony hag dance."

"Lie low with me, sweetheart, lie low."

The voices and shapes grew more animated as the rocking figure rocked faster. A large rat, appearing on her lap, cleaning its sticky filth laden whiskers as it held its self-steady. Long tail wrapped snake like round Maudy Jiller's stick thin forearm. A young girl with her head bent round the wrong way to look back over her shoulder sang as she danced around the cell.

"Mummy's stews are the devil's brew and her soups are little boy's bones. She goes out at night with a long sharp knife and bring the dead ones home."

Round and round the cell, the shapes and the noise danced, lurched and shouted until Maudy Jiller rocking faster than ever, lost her grip on the edge of the bench and rocked herself so far forward, she fell knees first onto the unyielding floor. The rat on her lap jumping quickly aside with an enraged squeal. The forward momentum of her fall overbalancing the kneeling figure to make her fall forward and sideways at the same time to land head first on the cell floor. The taut skin stretched over her forehead splitting open with a sickening thud. The impact knocking her senseless for several minutes and driving her personal demons back into the shadows of her misery. When she regained consciousness, Maudy Jiller couldn't understand why she was on her knees with her body bent double. The cell, cold and indifferent as always afforded her no explanation. Only the tearing sensation as the dried blood bonding her forehead to the stone floor pulled free and sent needles of pain through her injured head. A throbbing that joined the ache in her knees and lower back to force her to change position. The only thing was, Maudy Jiller was spent. Her limbs leaden and immovable. Every fibre of her being wrung out. Her emotions held between the finger and thumb of desperation, and squeezed till every ounce of feeling had been extracted. The spark of defiance that had bought her back from being beaten unconscious. The last reserves of inner strength that had seen her unbowed in court, gone. Leaving her an empty vessel. The woman who had endured much and fought back to overcome every challenge, was no more now than a worn-out shell. The trial and her manipulation of events had availed her nothing. Front page news forgotten tomorrow. The beast of Bonecreake was beaten and bowed. The crushing inevitability of her failure to protect her children, ripping the mother within to pieces.

"I did it all for you, my darlings. All for you to keep you safe."

Voices and shapes vaguely remembered moved slowly in her mind but they had no effect on her. Everything was gone. The stone floor gave no comfort yet she needed none. Nothing mattered anymore. Her pain was lessening as she rolled slowly sideways to end up lying on her side facing away from the cell door. The width of her shoulder pressed against the floor, leaving a space for her head to hang free. One upper arm held beneath her body as the adjoining forearm stuck out at awkward angle in front of her face. Her other arm lying across her body. Fresh drops of blood from the wound on her forehead slowly running down the side of her gaunt face. Pooling on the coarse material of the police issue smock dress.

"Are you tired, my angel?"

A voice soft and sweet asked in the darkness. Maudy Jiller's own voice soft and low with barely a rattle from her chest.

"Tired, tired and hungry. So hungry, Mummy. "

"Well, my little angel, we can't have an empty belly at bedtime. Mummy's bought you something nice to eat before you sleep."

A figure kneeled close over Maudy Jiller as she lay on the floor. A barely remembered face leaning down close to her own gaunt blood-streaked head.

"Just raise yourself up a little, sweetheart."

Maudy Jiller lifted her aching head slightly and propped herself upright from the waist with the arm lying over her body. The palm of her hand pressed against the hard floor to support her weight. Lifting the other arm trapped beneath her shoulders up until her forearm brushed against her face.

"That's it, now take a bite before you sleep. Your dreams will be all the sweeter for a little supper."

"Yes, Mummy."

Maudy Jiller bit down, just where her forearm met her wrist. Moving her forearm round with each bite to pierce the taut skin and bone to cut into the veins beneath. Blood spurting freely into her mouth, staining her face. Splashing her nose and blinding her as it filled the sunken eye sockets with sticky warmth.

"That's it. Mummy's here now and there's nothing to fear."

The voice muffled as Maudy bit down again. Twisting her head and forearm to give her teeth purchase on her stick thin arm. Gnawing like the rat in old Tom's privy gnawed at the bones of the stolen children.

"A little supper for my angel then it's off to sleep you go. There now that enough for your little belly. Snuggle down now, sweetheart."

Maudy Jiller let her bleeding forearm hang loose as she slumped down into the increasing pool of blood spreading across the cold floor.

"Sleep now, my angel. Mummy's here watching over you."

The blood flowing from the torn forearm slowed to a steady pulsing flow before it eased to an almost imperceptible trickle. Maudy Jiller's near lifeless body relaxing as life seeped away with every faint beat of the failing heart beneath her undernourished chest.

"Sleepy, Mummy."

Maudy Jiller's thin lips fluttered like butterfly wings as she lay dying. The taunts and threats from the monsters in her conscience powerless to hurt her. Every hardship she had ever known lying in the bloody pool around her. The stone floor indifferent to their story as it was to all else.

"Sleepy."

The lips stopped moving and the blood stopped flowing as Maudy Jiller's emaciated body drew a final rattling breath. Her last thought not of hunger and pain but of two little girls playing happily in the endless space where the land meets the sea, and the clouds fill the skies above the fish sheds and cottages of Bonecreake.

****

The same thoughts filled Constable Hollins mind as he let his imagination wander. The remnants of his evening meal on the plate lying on his lap, sat in his shirtsleeves and socks. His shirt unbuttoned at the collar. Uniform trousers blue against the red leather of the armchair. He mirrored hundreds of other men at their ease. Their day's work done and a satisfying meal under their collective belts. Allowing themselves a few moments of leisurely repose. In Constable Hollins case, his thoughts were on the marshes of Bonecreake and the North Sea beyond. The windswept landscape and skies that rolled on forever. Easing his shoulders deeper into the soft armchair. Constable Hollins allowed his mind's eye to sweep over the vista in his imagination.

There's a beauty to it when you look closely, he mused. *I should like to see it from the sea when the occasion presents its self. I daresay I could call upon the services of Isac Punce and ask his permission to come aboard and take a trip out around the wash area on his fishing boat. Yes. I will do that,* he told himself. *I shall make it my business to keep in touch with the people of Bonecreake and visit them in happier times when the fuss and clamour of the present has subsided.*

Constable Hollins smiled as he fancied a light breeze upon his face, the scent of fresh saltiness on the air. Immediately dispelled by a knocking on the door that jerked him back to reality with a start that sent his dinner plate crashing to the floor. Broken china and food scraps beneath his stockinged feet as he jumped upright.

Without in the darkening street Sergeant Crane hid a smile as his constable threw open the door. Braces hanging round his thighs. Boots under one arm, ready to rush to whatever emergency beckoned.

"Whoa, steady there."

Sergeant Crane stepped smartly aside as Constable Hollins's momentum carried him over the threshold and into the street.

"What is it, Sergeant? What's to do?"

Constable Hollins, flushed and disorientated at being summoned unexpectedly from his after-dinner nap, dropped his boots to the pavement and hurriedly struggled to tuck his shirt into his trousers and pull his braces over his shoulders. Dancing a strange jig on the spot as he struggled to dress himself.

"Calm yourself, Constable, calm yourself. Less haste, more speed. There's no need to strangle yourself. One dead body is quite sufficient for this evening, thank you."

"A body exclaimed the wriggling, Constable. What, where?"

Calmly Sergeant Crane ushered his constable back indoors, bending to pick up the discarded boots from the pavement as he did so.

"The doorstep is not the place to discuss Police business Hollins. In you go."

Steadier now and not a little embarrassed at his unseemly disorganisation. Constable Hollins faced his Sergeant as both men sat either side of the fireplace in the small sitting room.

Sergeant Crane leaning forward to speak, his injured arm resting across his lap.

"I was in the police station just catching up with some reports when the alarm was raised from the cells."

Constable Hollins felt his evening meal bubble in his stomach.

"Dear lord, don't tell me Maudy Jiller's escaped her cell and broken free?"

"In a manner of speaking Hollins. That's exactly what she has done, in spirit at least."

Constable Hollins's eyebrows raised quizzically.

"In spirit," he asked. "I don't understand. She's either a prisoner still or she isn't?"

"She dead, Hollins".

Sergeant Crane's words sent a shiver down Constable Hollins's spine.

"How? I don't understand. She was wasted and worn down certainly but she showed no sign of dying in court. Just the opposite in fact."

"Maudy Jiller died by her own hand, Hollins. Sergeant Crane's matter of fact delivery of the news made his next sentence almost brutal. She committed suicide in her cell by eating her own flesh through to the bone. Injuring herself so badly she bled to death before anyone knew what was happening."

For a moment Constable Hollins sat and stared into the empty fireplace. The enormity of Sergeant Crane's words sinking home. Maudy Jiller. Defiant to the last depriving the hangman of his breakfast and spitting in the eye of her accusers.

"How could this have happened? Surely a watch was set upon her?"

"No." Sergeant Crane sat back in the armchair. "Had she been transferred to prison to await execution? She would have been housed in the condemned cell. Two wardens would have sat on suicide watch within the cell until her sentence was carried out. As it was. Maudy Jiller had yet to face sentencing for murder, so she was housed in one of our own cells beneath the court."

"With no wardens present, Constable Hollins shook his head sadly. An oversight in procedure she took advantage off."

"As you say, Hollins. A procedural oversight. Although I doubt those responsible for her welfare whilst in custody, will draw little comfort from that. There'll be an inquiry of course and I daresay the wardens will be on the receiving end of some harsh words but that's about it. The prisoner mutilated her own body and died as a result of her actions. Her remains will be buried in un-consecrated ground as befits a suicide, and the passage of time will relegate this case to the annals of history. Remembered by those most affected. Forgotten by the majority, who don't want the horrors of the world hanging round their coat tails."

"I thought given your involvement with the case from the outset that you would like to be informed of this development. So I decided to call on you on my way home. It being but a small detour from my normal route. Now if you don't mind, I shall excuse myself and wish you a good evening. Mrs Crane will be anxious to see me home given I am not yet fully healed."

"Yes, of course."

Constable Hollins pushed himself upright out of his armchair as Sergeant Crane did likewise. The constable respectfully ushering his sergeant out the door to say his goodbyes from the doorstep.

"I don't think I will ever forget Maudy Jiller, Sergeant. In fact I am sure of it."

Sergeant Crane nodded in acknowledgement and turned about, disappearing from view as he walked off down the winding street. The burning pain and heat of spilled blood running down his forearm as Maudy Jiller's knife bit deep, etched into his memory.

"I won't forget her either, Hollins. Try as I might, I never shall."

For several months after her trial and subsequent suicide the case of Maudy Jiller was pored over and dissected by newspapers, pamphlets and penny dreadful alike. Her crimes and the grisly manner of her death, all grist to the literary mill that portrayed the unfortunate fishwife as hero or villain, depending on your choice of publication. For a while Bonecreake was besieged by the ghoulish. Clamouring to see the site where so much that was deemed unnatural had occurred. The Creaker's badgered and harried for details to such a degree that Captain Blades stationed a police constable in Bonecreake to keep order until the fuss died down. Which of course as Sergeant Crane had predicted, it did. Life moving on to leave the hamlet to its own desolate devices.

Constable Hollins. Now detective Hollins of the newly formed investigative branch of the service. Found himself unable to fulfil his promise to himself that he would return to Bonecreake. The life of a busy detective left little time for personal pleasures. Although he did correspond with Isac Punce and Mrs Potts the midwife on occasion.

The Creakers themselves went on about their business much as they always had. Putting Maudy Jiller to the back of their minds as they fished and scratched a living from the sea. For a while fish caught on a Bonecreake boat had fetched premium price but that didn't last long before the novelty wore off and things returned to normal.

These days there is little to show that anything untoward ever happened in this quite stretch of coastline. Of their own accord, the Creakers assembled together, watching in silent remembrance as Maudy Jiller's cottage was set alight and burnt to the ground. The ash and stone remaining after the fire carted away and dumped into the marshes. Sinking further down into the mud banks with each passing tide. Likewise old Tom's cottage and the two adjoining derelict cottages were demolished and the remnants of the privy still stacked at one end of the backyard burnt. The site of the stolen children's discovery left bare for nature to reclaim under a blanket of weeds and rough grass. Only the small cemetery on the edge of Bonecreake bears witness to the death and misery of Maudy Jiller's legacy. The grave markers fashioned by Eli Stone the gravedigger replaced with simple headstones to mark the final resting place of all those taken by the freezing winter. All except one are buried here. The exception being the youngest of Maudy Jiller's two daughters, who died on the day of her mother's arrest, her body lies unwanted and unloved by the majority of Creakers, somewhere in the open land behind her old home. The exact location known only by Mrs Potts the midwife, who true to her calling refused to abandon a child she had bought into the world. She was born a Creaker and died a Creaker, so she'll be buried a Creaker. I'll not condemn the daughter for the crimes of the mother. Her uncompromising stance supported by Reverend Ball who had blessed both the child and the ground she lay in. After the gravedigger Eli Stone had hacked a rudimentary grave from the rough terrain. The circumstances of the child's death fresh in both men's minds.

Now nothing remains of Maudy Jiller except a body mouldering in an unmarked grave. That and a young girl who spends her days shaking uncontrollably. Her eyes as lifeless as one of the many fish, filleted by her mother's slim-bladed knife. Lost somewhere inside herself, she rocks quietly to and fro. Her seat by the barred window shared with other unfortunates within the walls of the asylum. It's said she speaks to her mother in the long hours of the night and that her sister sometimes speaks with her too. The orderly's pay such ramblings no mind. The girl is quite and no trouble. They have others to care for who are not so inclined. Had they been less busy the orderly's might have been more concerned had they but listened closely to the shaking girl's words.

"I'm hungry, Mummy. Hungry enough to eat myself."

"Ssssh, little one," whispered the sticky whiskered rat curled up on her knee.

"Just take a small bite out of your fingers and save a little for me."

****

Ingram Content Group UK Ltd.
Milton Keynes UK
UKHW010951070423
419773UK00012B/1010